The Whytfield Investigation

The Policeman's Story

SW Fellows

The Whytfield Investigation

The Policeman's Story

First published in 2023

ISBN: 978-1-73998421-2

TAUK Publishing

DEDICATION

To my patient husband, family and friends for listening to further Whytfield tales—thank you.

CHAPTER 1

Adam Stagg sighed. As a police inspector, he'd seen dead bodies before, but none looked as fragile as this one. A woman lay on the floor, slumped forward on her knees. Her arms were askew at her side, like white twigs, and her feet had a purplish hue. She looked like a discarded pile of washing.

Stagg towered over a man in a brown crimplene suit who gently pulled some matted hair away from the girl's face.

"Not more than twenty-five, I would say, Stagg. I'll be able to confirm that later." The police pathologist examined the woman's face carefully.

Stagg nodded. "Thank you, Mr Yardley. And the cause of death?"

"Overdose, possibly. I'll give you all the details this afternoon. I've done all the photos, so I won't be long now."

A shaft of sunlight pierced through a chink in the curtains, slicing through the thick stagnant air of the flat, but it failed to illuminate the room. Stagg's glance swept around the place, taking in its contents. A shabby armchair and a ring-marked coffee table covered in crisp packets and cigarette papers filled the lounge area, and a half-empty bottle of lemonade stood on a cupboard in the kitchenette. As Stagg passed, cigarette ash floated through the air, looking for a place to settle. The bathroom was surprisingly clean, with a bottle of bleach and a toilet brush standing neatly at the side of the toilet.

"Anything unusual?"

Yardley put some samples in his case, removed his gloves, and stuffed them inside before snapping it shut. "No, not really. Shame. She was only a young girl."

"Yes. Thank you."

"See you later, Stagg."

Stagg nodded and sifted through some newspapers that were on the floor. He moved a pile of others on the top of an old sideboard and checked its cupboards. All they held were a jar of jam and a half-empty packet of digestive biscuits. No letters or bills—funny that. The sergeant's earlier conversation with the landlord hadn't revealed much either, only that her name was Jones.

Stagg went through to the bedroom, where the bed was neatly made. There were a few items in the wardrobe but no shoes or makeup, only a worn hairbrush. The bedroom door was propped open with a stuffed owl which Stagg moved to close the door. He found a lightweight brown coat hanging on the back of it, and, after going through the pockets, he found a few tissues, a red lipstick, a key and some loose change. Stagg popped these into his clean handkerchief and put them in his jacket pocket. There was also a card advertising The Iron Jim, a local boxing club.

Whoever had cleaned the flat had missed that. He reopened the door and replaced the owl, making sure he left everything as it was before the woman's death in case her boyfriend should return.

In the lounge, Stagg could see that the carpet underneath the corpse was stained, and he guessed she'd been in that position for a couple of days. Did she die alone? No needles or drugs had been found, even though there were a few marks on her arms. Who had been supplying her? Drugs had permeated into Whytfield since the sixties, but this was the first drug-related death that Stagg had been presented with. He shook his head and opened the front door to let in some fresh air. A policeman was standing outside.

"She can be moved now, and be careful, will you, Roberts?" Stagg was almost afraid the girl would break in two; she looked so fragile.

"Yes, Inspector Stagg."

***

Later, Stagg drove to The Iron Jim, which was only a few streets away. He parked across the road and watched the entrance to the club for several minutes. Young lads were coming in and out, and a thin man in a black tracksuit came outside and stood at the door. He looked up and down the street, dragging on a cigarette before going back inside. Stagg decided not to pay them a visit today. He'd wait to see what the pathologist would come up with first.

He returned to the station and had just started on his report when Assistant Chief Inspector Burns appeared.

"So, what's this I hear about an overdosed girl? You can't believe that can you, Stagg? Not here in Whytfield."

"I'm just waiting for the coroner's report, sir."

"Yes, of course you are. No leads to go on, then? No, I didn't think so. Well, don't let me disturb you, Stagg."

"Sir."

Stagg barely looked up. He didn't like Burns, and he had good reason. In the past eighteen months, he'd seen him humiliate young police officers and pass undue comments to the WPCs that worked at the station. Burns was a few years older than Stagg, but he could still remember him as a trainee officer who had been very ambitious.

Burns had joined the local golf club, which coincidentally was used by senior officers, including the chief inspector. Once Burns had got his sergeant's badge, he'd transferred to West Midlands Police and was quickly promoted. He'd just cracked a big drugs ring, and everyone was surprised when he'd transferred back to Whytfield, but he was to be the new Assistant Chief Inspector. It was obvious to everyone that he had his eye on the chief's job.

Stagg, relieved that Burns had gone, continued to work on his report when his phone rang.

"Hello! Ah, Mr Yardley…yes…overdose, eh…heroin? I see…yes, I'll look at your report in the morning…thank you…oh…going for a game of golf, are you? Yes…fresh air, that's what we all need…goodbye."

Stagg replaced the receiver. He could still smell the stagnant air of the flat on his clothes. He quickly finished his initial report and put it away. It was almost five o'clock.

***

Splatters of rain hurled themselves onto his windscreen. Stagg didn't think much golf would be played today—more like drinks in the clubhouse. He turned out of the station yard onto Whytfield High Street.

Although it was 1970, Whytfield had expanded little since World War Two. Stagg had lived in Whytfield all his life. It was an old market town in Shropshire, with a market cross on the square. A medieval stone church stood proudly at one end, opposite a large hotel, which had been specifically built to accommodate railway travellers. Due to the Beeching cuts, the once-busy railway station lay empty now, but there was talk of its buildings being developed. Pretty black and white cottages and shops spanned the streets, with many traders living above their businesses. On the outskirts of the town stood Whytfield Hall, occupied by Lord Whytfield and his family.

Stagg lived just out of town, on a private housing estate, about a mile from the police station. He'd picked a corner plot, as he wanted a big garden, and as Stagg turned onto his drive, he noted that the front lawn needed cutting. Stagg liked to keep it tidy. The shower of rain, thankfully, had been short, so he changed his clothes and fetched the lawnmower out of the shed. He would grab some tea later.

After mowing the grass, he cut some dead flower heads off his roses and decided to cut a few blooms to take indoors. Droplets of rain looked like tiny silver pearls amongst the pink petals, and the aroma was in direct contrast to the stale air of that flat. As he gathered half a dozen blooms, he remembered selecting similar ones for his fiancée Hazel. He took them into the kitchen and plunged them into some cold water. Maybe he'd take them to his mother later—she loved roses.

CHAPTER 2

The following morning, the pathologist's report landed on Stagg's desk. It was inconclusive regarding the woman's identity as there were no matching dental records on file. The pathologist had noted that she was about twenty-two, underweight, and had died from a heroin overdose some five days earlier. She had eaten crisps for her last meal and little else. There were several needle marks on her arms, and she had been taking contraception but had not been sexually active recently. She also had a small birthmark on the back of her neck, hidden underneath her hairline.

Stagg called Hudson, a WPC, into his office. She sprang to her feet and grabbed a notepad.

"Yes, sir? How can I help?"

"I'd like you to do some checks for me, please, on the Missing Persons' Register. Here is a copy of the coroner's report if you wish to take some details." Hudson scanned the report and scribbled down some notes. "I know it's a lot of work for you, Hudson. Now, she may be local, but she may not. I'm going to make a couple of other enquiries too. Okay? Good! Thank you, Hudson."

"Thank you, sir." She smiled and returned to her desk.

Stagg watched the WPC leave his office. If he were different, he would ask her out. She was pretty and intelligent, but he'd decided a long time ago that he wouldn't get involved with anyone again, not after Hazel. He shrugged on his coat and left the station.

Later, when Stagg arrived at The Iron Jim Boxing Club, he asked for the manager, but he wasn't there. A few young lads and an old chap, whose nose was squashed flat to his face, were getting ready to do some sparring. Stagg asked them whether a young girl had visited the gym lately.

"A girl? Here? Lawd, no! We don't get no girls coming in here. Why would they? This is a boxing club, mate, not the Women's Institute!" The man gave a toothless chuckle.

Stagg persisted, "You're sure?"

"Positive, mate. Now, if you don't mind, me and the lads have got some training to do. Alan, Chris! Come on, get in the ring."

Next, Stagg visited the block of flats where the woman's body had been found. He wanted to have a word with the landlord. After he tapped the door, it opened a crack, and the same stagnant smell hit Stagg.

"Hello. Yes?"

"I'm Inspector Stagg. May I come in?"

"No, you can't."

Stagg arched his eyebrows. "Why not?"

"Well, it's my mother, you see. She's got very bad nerves. It'd frighten her to death if she saw the police here."

"I'm sure. Now, what can you tell me about this dead girl? You found the body, didn't you?"

"Yes. But it wasn't anything to do with me. I hadn't seen anyone about there for a few days, and I'm entitled to go in and check my property, you know."

"Yes, I know. Now, did you touch anything in the flat?"

"No, I didn't. I saw her, and then I phoned the police."

"You phoned straight away?"

"Yes, I did."

"And you didn't remove anything from the flat, such as letters or anything?"

"No, I didn't. All I did was let myself in."

"Go on, tell me what you saw."

"Well, like I said, I stepped in just to check if they were still there. Sometimes tenants do a runner if they don't pay their rent. Anyway, I saw it was a bit messy, and I was going to check the bedroom when I saw her on the floor. Poor girl! I thought it was a heap of clothes at first."

"Did she live alone?"

"Yes, well, most of the time."

"What do you mean, most of the time?"

"Well, her friends used to come round, now and again."

"Did she have a regular boyfriend, and do you know any of her friends?"

"No. I mind my own business, thank you. The boyfriend paid upfront for three months, but it was coming to an end. I don't think he lived here."

"You don't know?"

"No, I told you, I mind my own business."

"The woman's name. Did you know that?"

"Only that her name was Jones. She was very quiet, and he did all the talking. I never saw her go out, to be honest."

"I see. Can you give a description of the man?"

"No, I didn't pay much attention. Anyway, when are you lot going to move out so I can rent the flat? I don't want to lose any money, you know!"

Stagg looked at the fat, balding man and politely replied, "I'll let you know. If you remember anything else, please get in touch. That's all for now, sir."

"Glad to be of service!" The door slammed in Stagg's face.

Stagg decided to set up surveillance on the flat, but after a week, no one visited, and he reluctantly allowed the landlord to rent out the flat. Stagg hoped that Hudson would come up with a name for the boyfriend. Chief Inspector Hughes hadn't commented on the case, but Stagg was sure that Burns was keeping him updated. Burns was hovering around Stagg's door when he returned to the station.

"Ah, Stagg, there you are! Anything more on that girl? You found nothing in the flat?"

"No, sir, only a card advertising a local boxing club called The Iron Jim."

"A boxing club? No link there, is there? I'd forget it if I were you, Stagg."

"You never know, sir. It could be important."

"I wouldn't waste your time, Stagg. You're grabbing at straws. Looks like this is going to be another "Unresolved' to me."

"Sir!" Stagg was glad when he'd gone.

A report of the woman's death was published by the local papers due to it being such an unusual occurrence in the town. Hudson's checks were inconclusive. Stagg was sure the girl had been used for prostitution. There were no shoes in the flat for the girl to wear, so she mustn't have gone out much, or it was possible that she may even have been imprisoned. Either way, Stagg was convinced she had been badly used and been kept more or less a prisoner in the flat. Unfortunately, no one came forward to identify her. The case was marked as 'Unresolved', as Burns had predicted, and the girl was buried in an unmarked grave in Whytfield cemetery.

***

For the rest of that summer, despite Burns' derogatory comments, Stagg successfully solved the usual run-of-the-mill offences: people creating disturbances late at night, usually after having too much to drink, a bit of shoplifting, and the odd thefts of bicycles.

Burns' unfounded criticism was starting to get Stagg down, not that anyone noticed, due to his professional manner. The summer weather was glorious, though, which was some compensation, and Stagg was glad to escape to his garden.

Stagg's roses were putting on a very fine display indeed, but he didn't feel they were as good as his grandads. He'd worshipped his grandfather and had enjoyed many visits as a youngster. He hadn't known, at the time, that they'd stayed there because of his father's drinking bouts. Stagg's childhood memories were bittersweet.

Initially, James and Moira Stagg had been very happily married, and James had always been ambitious. At one point, he'd considered taking his family to Australia using the subsidised travel package that the government offered. Stagg remembered how keen his father had been and that he had even got leaflets on it all.

"It would be great, Moira. All that sunshine! And I know I could do well, and we could buy a nice house."

"We've got a nice house, and you're doing well here, Jim. It's such a long way away."

"Yes, I suppose so. As long as we're together, that's the main thing. What do you think, Adam?"

"I don't know. I like playing out, and I could do that all the time there. I'd go brown as a berry! But I wouldn't like to leave grandad; that's the only thing. Could he come with us, Dad?"

"What? No! He wouldn't come, anyway. I want it to be just us."

"All right, Jim, we'll talk about it later."

They never did emigrate, and, looking back, Stagg supposed his father had been frustrated by his wife's lack of ambition. Instead, Jim Stagg worked hard at a local electrical factory and succeeded in working his way up to General Manager, but the hours were long, and the work was hard.

Jim started calling in for a drink at some of the local pubs on his way home. It was just for him to relax a bit, he'd told Moira, but the drinking bouts became more frequent, and soon he demanded that drink be kept in the house.

Moira supported her husband in his career, often throwing dinner parties for Jim's boss and his wife. Mr Owen, the owner, had encouraged Jim to join the golf club, as it made good business sense and he could make a lot of useful 'friends'. Jim Stagg was drinking quite heavily now but disguised it well in public. Stagg remembered the terrible quarrels that his parents had, often resulting in a trip to his grandads. Once, he heard Bob Lloyd whisper to his mother, "You're a fool to stay with him, Moira."

Whilst roses brought happy and sad memories back to Stagg, he'd learnt to adapt to the pain as he grew into a man. He'd promised himself that he wouldn't allow his frustrations push him towards alcoholism, so throughout the summer, he turned to his garden to clear his mind and to take his mind off his work.

All too soon, the summer came to an end, and the leaves on the trees had turned into lovely shades of gold and russet. The school children trailed through their crunchy remnants as they reluctantly returned to their lessons. As Stagg was going through town one autumn morning, the traffic slowed to allow some horse-drawn caravans through. It was the group of gipsies who stayed on the outskirts of Whytfield each autumn for the potato picking.

As Stagg waited in the traffic, he saw the gipsy leader walking at the side of the first caravan. He wore a black trilby and a black jacket. His skin was weather-beaten and brown, but his eyes were as black as coal. He caught sight of Stagg and put his hand up to him to wave. Stagg nodded back. He had known Ralph for years, and his family were good workers and harmless enough. There were four horse-drawn caravans, followed by two modern ones pulled by cars. '*Even gipsy life was changing,*' Stagg thought as he drove to the station.

***

Not long after, on a Thursday night, a garage owner was threatened by two men who pushed him down to the floor. A substantial amount of money was taken, and the robbers left no evidence behind. Thankfully, the owner was just shaken, but he couldn't give any kind of description of the men, as they were wearing stockings over their faces, and he hadn't seen the car that they were driving.

"Any leads, Stagg?" Burns snapped the following day.

"Not yet, sir," Stagg replied.

"Have you visited the gipsy site yet?"

"No, sir. I have no reason to." Burns snorted and shook his head. "I'm following all the usual procedures, sir, and…."

"Yes, I'm sure you are, Stagg. Everyone knows you follow procedures. Slow and steady. Let's hope you're fruitful this time."

Stagg's stomach was churning. He didn't appreciate Burns' booming voice, especially in the police station. He didn't like Burns, and he knew the feeling was mutual.

Hudson appeared at the doorway. "I've done those checks for you, sir, as you requested." She glared at Burns, who looked her up and down.

"Glad you're helping him, love. He needs it."

"Thank you, Hudson. Will there be anything else, sir?" Stagg said quietly.

Burns glared at Stagg, who, with eyes like polished steel, returned an equally serious look.

"No, I'll leave you two to it. At this rate, you'll be back on the beat, Stagg! That's all!" He nodded at Hudson, whose cheeks were flushed.

When he'd gone, Stagg asked, "Well? Anything, Hudson?"

"I'm afraid not, sir."

Stagg gripped his pencil so hard under his desk that he heard it crack. He knew Burns seemed to influence senior officers, but he also knew that he couldn't be demoted, not without a very good reason. All he could hope for was that Burns would move on to another station. Stagg didn't bear grudges as a rule, but he had his own reasons for disliking Burns.

Stagg hadn't exactly enjoyed discovering that Burns had been carrying on with his fiancée, Hazel, all those years ago. Not that Burns knew this was why Stagg ended his engagement. He had blamed their careers. She was a trainee nurse then, and Stagg was a constable.

After they'd split up, Stagg had focused on his work. It had helped ease the pain. He couldn't help feeling sorry for Hazel, though, when she'd found out that Burns was married with a family. The whole episode was upsetting for everyone except Burns.

Stagg promised himself he wouldn't put himself through that pain again, so he'd worked hard. He wasn't overly ambitious like his father, but he took pride in doing a good job. Whilst he followed procedures, he was no fool. He couldn't help wondering whether the dark nights of the oncoming winter would assist these robbers.

CHAPTER 3

A few weeks later, Stagg was working late when there was a report of a hit-and-run. What made matters worse was that a little girl had been knocked over, and it sounded like she was in a critical condition.

Stagg drove to the scene straightaway, but there was little to see. A policeman was checking the road for collision marks, and some people were still standing nearby. Stagg nodded to one of them.

"Did you see anything?" he asked a man in a sleeved shirt.

"No. But we heard Josie scream. It was awful! We were just having our tea, weren't we, Elsie?"

A woman wearing a headscarf tugged at her coat. "Yes. When we heard the commotion, we ran down the lane. Joe and Vera were there already. Poor Nora! Her leg looked bad. Whoever was driving that car should be strung up. They didn't stop, you know. Poor thing! We've got little Josie here with us. She's in our house, playing with our son Johnny. Joe and Vera have gone to the hospital with Nora in the ambulance."

"Josie?"

"Nora's sister. She's so upset!" The woman whipped a handkerchief from her sleeve and sniffed into it before stuffing it back. Her husband placed his arm round her back.

"Okay. Come on now. Don't get upset. We'd better get back home," Tom said.

"Yes, but it could have been our Johnny, Tom."

"I know, but thankfully it wasn't. Poor Nora. Sorry, we can't be of much help."

"That's all right, sir. No one else saw anything?"

"No, they were the only ones out playing."

"What time did it happen, do you think?"

"About half past six, wasn't it, Elsie?"

"Yes, that's right. It was just starting to get dark."

"I see. And you didn't hear anything before you heard Josie shout?"

"No, I was too busy cooking the fish. We always have fish on a Friday, you see."

"Okay, well, thank you both for your help."

"That's all right. I hope you catch them; I really do. Maybe it's one of those gipsies!" the man growled.

"I'll try my best to catch whoever's responsible, sir."

As Stagg walked back to his car, another vehicle pulled up, and a man jumped out, holding a camera with a flash.

"Are you the police? There's been a hit-and-run, hasn't there? What happened?"

Stagg gritted his teeth. "Yes, barely an hour ago. We have no information yet." He opened his car door.

"Okay, sir. I'll have a word with these people here, then." The reporter then ran after the couple Stagg had just spoken to, who were walking back to their house.

Stagg started his car. He hated the press. They had their uses, of course, but he viewed them as more of an aggravation. He drove to the Whytfield Major Hospital and went to the main reception desk to get directions to the children's ward. As he approached the ward, he saw a couple sitting outside in the corridor, and Stagg could see they were upset. He sat down next to them.

"Excuse me, but are you Mr and Mrs Davies? I'm from the police; I'm Inspector Stagg. How is your daughter?"

The woman wept into a scarf that she clutched to her face, and her husband wrung his hands in front of him. "The doctors are with her now. They think…oh…they think she might lose her leg because it was so twisted!" she gasped. Her husband put his arm around her, and they clung tightly to each other. His eyes were watery with tears.

"Now, we don't know that for sure yet. That's what they're checking now. Come on, now, there, there." Mrs Davies looked up and gripped his hand. She offered a half smile.

Stagg sat down. "I'm sorry. Has she said anything?"

"No. She was unconscious when we saw her," Mr Davies said, looking down. Just then, the ward door opened, and two male doctors came out.

"Well, we've examined Nora's leg," one doctor began, "and we're confident it can be saved, but Nora will need all her strength. It's a very bad break, I'm afraid, and we're not sure yet whether she'll need surgery. That's all we can say for now."

Mrs Davies, who had stood up when the doctors had appeared, flopped back down on the chair. She whispered, "But she is going to be all right, isn't she, Doctor?" Her face was white, and both parents held their breath, waiting for the doctor's reply.

"The next twenty-four hours are critical. I'm sorry. While she's a strong and healthy girl, this has been a huge shock to her body. All being well, she should start recovery tomorrow. She'll need to go into traction as soon as possible, and we're arranging for that to be done tomorrow. She'll be under anaesthetic, of course, then in plaster. Then she'll need physiotherapy and do exercises to improve her leg, but it's going to be a long job. We can't say if all this will leave her with an impaired walk at this stage."

"So, she'll have a limp?" Mr Davies asked.

"We don't know yet. It will depend on how well she heals," the other doctor said.

"Thank you, Doctor. Can we go in to see her now?" Mrs Davies asked.

"Yes, of course, but she's sedated, so she mightn't know you're here. You must be very quiet, and she's not to be upset. She's to go to X-ray soon. As I said, the next few hours are vital to her recovery. Come with me."

Mrs Davies wiped her eyes, and both parents, afraid of what they might see, took a deep breath before they tip-toed into the ward. Stagg asked one of the doctors if Nora had said anything about the accident.

"No. She was drifting in and out of consciousness, so she said very little other than cry. I'm afraid her life is in the balance. Sorry, but I must get back."

"Of course, Doctor. Thank you."

Stagg sat down and waited for a while outside the ward. He peeped through the door's small window and saw curtains pulled around a bed in the corner. He turned away and felt very angry. He'd never known a hit-and-run to happen in Whytfield. Someone must have seen something. He sprang forward, almost cat-like, and left the hospital.

As he drove home, rain clattered against his windscreen, drumming his angry thoughts into a fury. He ran into his cold kitchen and made himself a coffee. It was going to be a long night.

Early the following morning, Stagg phoned the hospital and was relieved to hear that Nora Davies had survived the night and only needed traction, not surgery, on her leg. It still meant months of being in plaster for the poor girl. Meanwhile, Stagg planned on doing small house-to-house enquiries, just in case someone had seen the speeding car.

Almost as soon as he arrived at the station, Sergeant Roberts informed him of a robbery at a factory a couple of miles out of town.

"A substantial amount of money was taken when the owner was closing the offices. He was emptying the safe when two men burst in and threatened him with a gun. He waited a few minutes after they'd left and then phoned the police, sir."

"What time was this, Roberts?"

"About five-thirty, sir."

"I see. Okay, thank you, Roberts." Stagg sat down. Hudson tapped the door of his office. "Yes? Oh, hello, Hudson." He'd half-expected it to be Burns.

"Morning, sir. I just wondered if you'd seen the paper this morning. I've brought you a copy. It covers the accident last night."

"They're on the ball, aren't they?" Stagg scanned the front page, which read: *POLICE NEED YOUR HELP!* "Oh, great! Just what I need! Thanks, Hudson."

"I thought I'd let you know before anyone else does, sir." As if on cue, Stagg's phone rang. It was the chief inspector.

"Stagg? What's all this nonsense in the papers? *'The Police need your help!'* What the devil are you doing talking to the press? We conduct our own investigations!"

"I didn't say anything to the press other than I didn't have anything to report, sir."

"Well, you shouldn't have said anything at all, Stagg, least of all to the press!"

"Yes, sir. I understand that I…."

"Good! Well, oh, just get on with your work, Stagg!"

"Yes, sir," Stagg said, but the chief inspector had already slammed his phone down. Stagg replaced his receiver carefully and sighed, forgetting Hudson was still at the doorway.

"Are you all right, sir? I can make you a cup of tea if you like." She smiled.

"What? Oh, no thanks, Hudson. Not just now." He stood up. "If we do get any reports from the public about this accident, follow procedure, please. Names, addresses, the usual thing. I'm just popping out."

"Yes, of course, sir."

Stagg nodded. He knew Hudson always did a thorough job.

***

The Davies' were surprised at seeing Stagg, and Mrs Davies asked him in.

"Would you like a cup of tea?" She wiped her hands on her apron, turned to her daughter and said, "Go upstairs now, Josie. There's a good girl." A girl with long plaits ran up the stairs. "We've kept her off school after all the upset yesterday. She didn't get to sleep till late last night, did she, Joe?"

Joe Davies was sitting at a small table that had a blue and white checked cloth on it. He nodded to Stagg as he stirred his cup of tea.

"No, poor girl. The neighbours looked after her for us. They told us that she thought we were going to shout at her, you know. She said it was all her fault. She had cried and cried till she couldn't cry no more. Then she just fell asleep, suddenly, they said. Just like when she was a baby, I suppose."

Stagg sat down. “I understand this mightn’t be an ideal time to ask a few questions, but I wondered whether Nora had described the car or driver. Anything at all, really.”

“No, she was sedated, so she didn’t say anything, and we didn’t either. We held her hand all night, though. We left about five o’clock this morning, didn’t we, Joe?” Vera Davies sat down.

“Yes, we did. But they said she was better when we phoned at nine o’clock. She’s in traction now, and we’re going in to see her this afternoon. They said she should have come round a bit by then.”

“I’m sorry, Mr Davies. Has her sister said anything about it all?”

“No. Josie’s so upset about it. Blames herself, doesn’t she?” Mr Davies nodded to his wife.

“Didn’t she say it was a green car, Joe?” Mrs Davies asked.

“Yes, I think she did. I don’t really want to ask her too much today because she’s still very upset.”

“Yes, of course. Did Josie tell you anything else, sir?” Stagg persisted.

“Only that when Nora had been knocked over, her shoe had somehow got caught on the bumper of the car.” Joe Davies wrung the tablecloth in front of him.

“Do you know, they dragged her for a hundred yards down the road. A hundred yards! My girl! It’s a wonder she’s got any skin left on her back. They must have known they'd hit something. I'd like to drag whoever it was down the road and see how they like it!”

Mrs Davies, who was sniffling in her hanky, handed her husband a tea-towel. He quickly wiped his face.

"Yes, sir. I see." Stagg said. "It is a very sad state of affairs. Let's hope that Nora makes a full recovery. I'll make a few notes for my report. You'll have to make a statement; it's procedure."

"I think you'd be better off trying to catch who did it, if you don't mind my saying! Have you seen the paper? At least they're on the ball, anyway," said Mr Davies.

"Joe! Don't be rude! The policeman's only trying to help."

"Oh, all right, Vera. Sorry, I'm just upset by it all. I suppose we could ask Nora tomorrow, maybe, and then we could phone you if she says anything."

Stagg stood up and smiled briefly. "I understand. Yes, that would be very helpful. Thank you. Here's my number." Stagg handed him a piece of notepaper and stepped to the door. "Anything at all, remember! It's surprising what children do notice, you know."

"Yes, it is. Have you got children too, sir?" Mrs Davies asked. Mr Davies quickly nudged his wife in disapproval.

"No. I'm not married. Well, goodbye."

Stagg got into his car and watched the couple quietly close the door. He glimpsed Josie's face peeping at him through an upstairs window, but as soon as she knew he had seen her, she dived out of view. He swung his car around in the small lane flanked by high hedges. This was certainly not a lane for speeding down.

***

On his way back to the station, Stagg visited the Baines factory where the robbery occurred. It was amongst a small group of factories just outside Whytfield. He was shown into the manager's office, and a tall, middle-aged man dressed in a smart suit entered the room. He sat down behind his desk.

"Good evening. Now, I take it you're in charge of this business about the robbery?" he asked.

"Yes, I'm Inspector Stagg. Are you the owner of the factory? Mr Baines?"

"Yes, I certainly am, and I want those robbers caught and caught quickly!"

"Yes, sir. Can you tell me what happened?"

"I've told your constables all this. I really don't have time to go through it again!"

"I just want to clarify a few points. How much money was taken, sir?"

"I don't have to tell you that! Let us just say it was a considerable amount," the owner snapped.

"Hundreds? Thousands?"

"How dare you! It's none of your business!"

"You'll need to report it to your insurance company, sir."

"Fine. It was around ten thousand pounds."

"How many men were there? Two, three?"

"Two, and they were armed."

"Did you see a gun, sir?"

"Well, no, I didn't. But one of them pushed it in the small of my back just as I was emptying the safe."

"How often do you empty the safe, sir?"

"Every Friday night, before I go home. I don't like leaving money on the premises over the weekend."

"Did you have more money in the safe than usual?"

"Yes, I did, as a matter of fact. I'd drawn some additional cash out of the bank for some business I was going to sort out on Monday over in Birmingham. Of course, I won't be doing that now." The factory owner took out a cigarette from a silver cigarette case and lit it. He put the case back in his inner coat pocket.

"How many people knew about your trip to Birmingham?"

"Oh, only the staff in the office, but they didn't know how much I was going to take with me. I don't divulge that much information to my staff." The man drew on his cigarette.

"You're sure?"

"Well, of course, I'm sure! What did you say your name was? Stagg? No relation to that Jim Stagg, are you? He used to come to the golf club. Anyway, I play golf with some of your senior officers, including the chief inspector and his assistant, Burns, so I'd watch my step if I were you."

Stagg ignored the question about his father and pressed on. "Of course, sir. So, just to recap, you were emptying the safe when two men approached you from the rear. They thrust what you thought was a gun in your back and told you to lay flat on the ground. Is that correct?"

"Yes, yes! I've told you."

"Yes, sir. Then what happened?"

"They emptied the safe and told me to stay where I was, or they'd blow my head off! So, obviously, I didn't move until I heard their car leaving the car park. I wasn't going to take any chances."

"Did you see the car, sir, or get their registration number?"

"No, I didn't. It was a dark car, I think. But other than that, I really can't say."

"Were you alone here on Friday night? No other staff present?"

"No, no one."

"Is there anything else you can remember, sir?"

"No. I told you. That's it! Hadn't you better get on and try to catch those thieves? Is there any chance of getting my money back?" He stubbed his cigarette in his ashtray, twisting it into almost nothing.

"I don't know, sir. But I'll be in touch as soon as I have any further information. Goodbye."

"Huh! I suppose that will have to do, won't it? Goodbye."

Stagg drove back to the station, mulling over the violent events of the last few days. A hit-and-run and two robberies. Was there a link?

CHAPTER 4

The chief had been informed of the factory robbery and angrily insisted that Stagg needed some help. Stagg was sure that Burns had embellished the fact that there was little to go on, even though investigations were ongoing.

"Another 'Unresolved' case, Stagg. The chief won't look too kindly on this, I'm sure." Inspector Burns smirked.

Stagg felt his body stiffen in anger, but he said nothing. He knew Burns was watching for the slightest excuse to tittle-tattle to the chief inspector. There was also a rumour going around the station that the chief was looking for someone to train up a fresh and keen police recruit who happened to be his nephew. Stagg hoped he wasn't going to palm him off on him. As if he didn't have enough to do!

Stagg was busy getting together the details of the robbery when he was summoned to the inspector's office. "*What now?*" Stagg thought and trundled down the corridor, nodding to WPC Hudson. If he had been ten years younger, he might have considered asking her out. Not now, though, not after all that business with Hazel. Besides, he was too busy with work but not too busy to acknowledge the young constables, especially the

WPCs. He knew they were often asked to do a tremendous amount of tedious work, for which they received very little gratitude.

WPC Jones watched Pamela Hudson smiling to herself as Stagg headed down to the chief's office. She whispered, "Oh, looks like old Stagg's in the doghouse again!"

"What? Oh, I don't know. And he's not that old," Hudson said. She grabbed a pile of papers that were on her desk.

"Well, I heard he's going to have a bit of help, some relation of the chief's. I feel sorry for them, anyway."

"Why?" said Hudson, looking up from the paperwork.

"Because Stagg's so boring, Pamela! He only ever talks about work. I did hear that he was engaged once and gave it up to follow his career in the police."

"Well, that's his job, isn't it?" Hudson wrestled a piece of paper out of the pile.

"That's right; you defend him." Jones laughed.

"I don't know what you mean!" Hudson scribbled some notes on her pad.

Hudson had assisted Stagg many times in the past. But she had to admit that she barely knew anything about his private life other than he was single and was about forty. She liked his methodical approach to work and noticed the quiet, determined look that came into his eyes when he was placed under pressure. But perhaps he would appreciate some extra help.

In the chief's office, Stagg saw a young fair-headed man sitting, quite relaxed, on one of the chief's armchairs. His stomach sank.

"Sir?" Stagg smartly said as he entered.

"Sit down, Stagg." The chief motioned towards a chair. "This is my…this is Wilkins, Stagg. I want him to assist you with your work." Stagg glanced at the young man who was keenly observing him. He nodded.

"I see, sir." Stagg sat down.

"Well? Have you anything to say?"

"No, sir." There was no point.

"Good! Excellent! No more leads on these burglaries, I suppose. No? I thought not! Well, off you go then. Stagg will instruct you, Wilkins, I'm sure! That's all!"

Stagg and Wilkins walked back down the corridor until they reached Stagg's office. Wilkins glanced at Stagg.

"Sir?"

"Yes? What is it?" Stagg was keen to get back to his paperwork.

"How do you want me to help you, sir?"

"You can do some checks for me. I'll show you. Sit down."

Wilkins sat and looked around. It was an extremely tidy office and looked almost unused. The only clue was the inspector's nameplate on the door. A dark-headed WPC entered the doorway, but she hesitated on seeing Wilkins.

"Excuse me, sir, but I've done some of those checks from the door-to-doors for you. It's going to take a while, though. One vehicle seems to crop up a couple of times, a green Ford Cortina, sir. There were a couple of reports of one speeding in that area at around that time."

"Good, Hudson. Any description of the driver?"

"No, sir. It was dark at the time of the accident."

"Right. Thanks, Hudson. This is Wilkins. Can you help Hudson, Wilkins? She'll show you what you'll need."

"Certainly, sir!" Wilkins jumped up.

Hudson smiled. "If you'd like to come with me?" She marched ahead down the corridor.

Wilkins stood up. "But sir, I thought I was going to do some real police work with you, sir."

"Well, you can start by following my orders, Wilkins."

"Sir!"

Wilkins followed Hudson out, and Stagg watched him go. That had gotten rid of him for a while, at least. He sat back in his chair. A Cortina, eh? Well, if anyone could check out all the facts, it was WPC Hudson, but there were a lot of Ford Cortinas out there. He was wondering whether he should visit Nora Jones again when Sergeant Roberts knocked on his door.

"Sir? There's a chap at the front desk saying he knows who that girl is. The one who died from the overdose in the summer, sir."

"Really? Thank you, Roberts. Show him into the interview room, please. Thank you." Stagg grabbed his notepad and shouted across to Wilkins. "Come on then, Wilkins, if you want to see some real police work! Just observe, please. I'll fill you in later."

He hurried down the corridor to Interview Room One, followed by Wilkins. They entered to find a man seated, clutching a tweed cap. Stagg introduced himself and Wilkins.

"And you are?" Stagg asked.

"Harold Jones. I've come forward to identify the young woman you found last year. The one with the birthmark. She's my daughter."

"I see. What was her name?"

"Jennifer, well Jenny we used to call her, for short. Her full name is Jennifer Louise Jones."

"When did you last see Jennifer, sir?"

"Oh, that would be a couple of years ago, in Oswestry. We only caught sight of her near the market, but then we couldn't find her after that."

"So, she wasn't living with you?"

"No, she'd moved out by then. With him—her boyfriend. Not that we met him, me and Beryl. He always used to pick her up in his car. He never came in the house. Filled her head with all sorts of nonsense, he did! And she'd been such a sweet girl, quiet and shy, you know?"

Stagg nodded. "So, when did she leave home?"

"About three years ago, I think. She was never the same after she left. Once, she phoned. Once!" Harold screwed up the cap he was holding, and he looked down. "Beryl was very upset over it all. I don't know. All her spirit seemed to have gone like a candle being blown out. She was never the same. Didn't eat much. You know how women are when they get upset."

"Yes." Stagg waited.

Harold let out a long sigh. "Two years after Jenny left, Beryl was diagnosed with a stomach ulcer, and that knocked her about a bit. But then it changed to cancer this year, and they said at the hospital that nothing could be done for her. She died two weeks ago."

"I'm sorry about your wife, Mr Jones."

"Yes, well...." Harold sniffed. "So, I thought I'd better come forward and identify Jenny."

"Why didn't you come earlier, sir?"

Harold's eyes stretched, and he leant forward. "I couldn't, don't you see? I didn't want to chance Beryl finding out. It could have got in the papers, and it would have broken her heart, for sure, it would. She didn't deserve that, not on top of what she was going through! She was so ill, sir." He blew his nose loudly in a white handkerchief, then whispered, "I just couldn't do it to her."

"I understand, Mr Jones. Now, if you can give me a few more details about your daughter?"

"The papers said that it was an overdose. Is that right?""

"I'm afraid so."

"Silly girl!" Harold clasped his handkerchief and shook his head.

"Did you know her boyfriend's name?"

"No, she wouldn't tell us. Said it was none of our business. She seemed to change into a stranger overnight."

"I see."

"I want to arrange a headstone for her, you see. Her mother would have wanted that for her." He wiped his eyes.

"Of course."

After Stagg had taken his address details, he told Harold Jones where Jenny was buried. When Stagg had finished, Harold reached into his pocket, pulled out a faded photo, and showed it to Stagg.

"See! This is what she was like before. We'd gone over to Porthmadog for a little holiday."

Stagg looked at the happy, healthy dark-headed girl in a swimming costume, standing next to a lady, presumably Beryl Jones. It was a far cry from the scrap of a girl he'd seen in the flat. He handed the photo back and nodded to Mr Jones.

"Thank you, sir, for coming forward. I'll advise the coroner, and he'll forward the death certificate. Wilkins, can you show Mr Jones out, please?"

"Yes, sir. This way Mr Jones."

"Thank you. Goodbye, sir."

Stagg watched as Harold Jones followed Wilkins down the corridor. Sad to see how some people seem to experience such trauma in their lives. He returned to his office and was soon joined by Wilkins.

Wilkins asked, "So, who was Jennifer Jones, sir?" Stagg filled him in with all the details of the woman's unexplained death.

"It was very sad to see, Wilkins. She was so thin. Terrible waste."

"Sir. At least we know who she is now, though. What do we need to do now?"

"I just need to complete a report that goes to the coroner's office."

Stagg asked Wilkins to retrieve the original case notes from the police archives. When he returned, Stagg went through the documents and the reporting procedure. He hoped that the fresh-faced young man was taking it all in. Whilst the information had solved the woman's identity, it did little to ease the sour taste in Stagg's mouth, but at least it was some sort of closure.

***

The following day, as Stagg had half-expected, Burns was at his door. "So, that dead woman's been identified then?"

"Yes, her father came forward."

"Where's he been till now? I hope you gave him a telling-off, Stagg!"

"His wife's been extremely ill, sir. He didn't want to upset her."

"Yes, well, that's no excuse! Did he say anything?"

"About what, sir?" Stagg's eyes glinted like steel.

"About drugs, man! Have I got to spell everything out for you, Stagg?"

"No, nothing about drugs, sir."

"Lucky for you, he came forward, what with your record of unresolved cases. God!" Burns left the office.

"Yes, bloody, sir!" Stagg muttered under his breath. He jumped when Hudson appeared in the doorway.

"Tea, sir? I'm just making some."

"That would be great, Hudson, thanks." Stagg smiled. She was a kind girl.

CHAPTER 5

A few days later, Stagg visited Nora Davies at the hospital. He knew she was doing well, as he'd regularly tracked her progress. He hoped she might be able to tell him what happened. He'd left Wilkins continuing the car checks with Hudson. It was important that he learnt the correct procedure.

When Stagg arrived at the ward, Mr Davies was sitting outside. He stood up when he saw the policeman approach. "Hello there," he said, nodding. "The wife and Josie are on the ward at the moment. They only allow two visitors at a time, you see."

"Yes. How is Nora?"

"Better, thank you, but it's going to be a long job. She was lucky she didn't need surgery, only traction. They reckon it could take as long as twelve months, you know."

"Oh, dear. I'm sorry to hear that. Well, let's hope she gets better soon; that's the main thing. I wondered if she'd said anything else about the accident, Mr Davies?"

"Well, no, not really. If I'm honest, we've avoided talking about it to save upsetting her."

"Yes, I see. Do you think she'd be up to my having a word with her? I won't upset her, I promise."

The child's father looked at this tall man with thick, black hair and blue-no-grey eyes. Stagg smiled at him, and Joe Davies knew that this was a man who could be trusted.

"Yes, I think that'll be all right," he said, getting up.

"I won't stay long, only a couple of minutes. Thank you."

When they entered the ward, Mrs Davies and her daughter looked up. Mrs Davies smiled but looked enquiringly at her husband. Joe whispered, "Now look, this chap wants to have a chat with Nora, so you two can wait outside a minute. He won't be long." He nodded to his wife and Josie, and they crept out while Joe remained with Stagg.

Nora was ensconced in a bed covered in pure white starched sheets. Stagg looked at her small dark head amongst the pillows and saw two large brown eyes watching him curiously as he sat near the bed.

"Hello, Nora. How are you today?" Stagg smiled and looked deep into the girl's eyes.

"Are you a doctor?" whispered Nora.

"No, I'm a policeman," Stagg whispered back.

"Where's your uniform?"

"Nora! Don't be cheeky!" her father said. Stagg ignored him.

"Well, the police decided to send one of their special policemen as you're a very special girl."

"Oh, that's nice of them, isn't it?"

"Yes. Now, they sent me here, Nora, to test your memory. You know, like the teacher does in school."

"Like our times tables? I like times tables." The girl smiled.

"Yes, just like those. It is a test to see how brave you are. Are you brave, Nora?" The girl thought about it for a few seconds.

"Yes, I think so." She beckoned Stagg to come nearer. "You haven't found out about me going into old Mr Smith's garden to pinch some apples off his trees, have you? I'm not in trouble, am I? They were only apples, and I was the brave one!"

"No, you're not in trouble. But maybe ask Mr Smith next time. So, how were you brave?" Stagg asked.

"Well, none of the others would go, but I did. I climbed right to the top, nearly. That was brave, wasn't it?" Tears ran down Joe Davies' face when he heard her whispers. He wondered if she'd ever be able to climb trees again. Stagg smiled.

"Yes, that was, Nora. Now, I know it's not nice for you to remember, but I want you to tell me what happened on the day you hurt your leg."

"Okay, but I don't remember much after that car came." She took a deep breath, and for a moment, Stagg thought she would cry, but instead, she continued. "Well, me and Josie were playing on the lane. We were on our bikes, and Mum said we had five minutes left to play before we had to go in. But it wasn't really dark, so we went to the bottom of the road "cos it's easier to ride there." Nora glanced at her father. "We're only allowed as far as there, but no further, and we don't talk to strangers." She smiled at Joe Davies, seeking his approval, and he smiled back.

"Yes, very good, Nora. What happened next? Take your time; I'm in no hurry." Stagg leaned forward.

"We thought we heard something coming down the lane. I thought it was a motorbike, and I don't like them. So, I decided to run back home. I jumped off my bike and made a dash for it across the road. But it wasn't a bike; it was a car, and I don't know, it all went funny after that." Nora fidgeted her fingers on the starched sheets, and her father reached out and held them.

"Very good, Nora. You've done very well for remembering so much. Thank you." Stagg nodded. Nora looked at the policeman and smiled a toothy grin.

"Oh, and it was a green car, by the way. Have I passed the test?"

"Yes! You scored ten out of ten." Stagg laughed.

"Good! I like tests."

"Do you remember anything else about the car?"

"Not much. Only that it was very noisy and big and boxy."

"Boxy?"

"Yes, a bit square. I think it had square lights, not round ones like we've got on our car. We've got a Ford Consul, you know, haven't we, Dad?"

"Yes, that's right." Joe Davies chuckled.

"Very good, Nora. Well done for remembering so much." Stagg stood and thanked them again before leaving the ward. He met Mrs Davies in the corridor.

"Everything all right?" she asked, holding Josie's hand.

"Yes, everything's fine."

"From what she's just said, it was inevitable that the car would hit her. It was going too fast, far too fast, so it wasn't your fault, Josie."

"Some youngsters, I suppose?" Mrs Davies asked.

"Maybe. We'll do our best to track the driver down. Goodbye, Mrs Davies, Josie."

Stagg left the ward and headed back to the station. As they went back into the ward, Josie Davies asked her mother what 'inevitable' meant. She was going to tell her mother that there were two men in the car, not one, but her mother told her to be very quiet in the ward, so she was.

***

Back at the station, Stagg's enquiries on the car were fruitless. A spot check had been done on all green cars in the Whytfield area, and all of them were legitimate, and they hadn't had any recent accidents. Stagg was studying a map of the local area when Wilkins tapped his door.

"Yes, what is it?"

"Well, sir, I've been running the checks on cars with Hudson for a few days now. I just wondered if I could do something else, sir, you know, real police work. Like we did before."

Stagg looked up from the map. "Real police work? So, you think WPC Hudson doesn't do real police work? Checks need to be done in all police work, Wilkins, and the sooner you learn that, the better!" Stagg snapped.

"Yes, but sir, I have been doing them for ages now, and I'm supposed to be helping you. My unc…the chief inspector assigned me to assist you, not sit at a desk all day with a WPC!"

"Well, you'd better get used to it, Wilkins, because checks need to be done, whether they're with a WPC or with me. I'm sure you learnt in your training days. Can I stress that the work that the WPCs do at this station is very important and isn't to be underestimated? Now, I suggest you return to your work, Wilkins!"

Burns appeared at the doorway. "Any leads, Stagg? Have you checked those gipsies? I hope you're training your new helper well to follow the correct procedure. We don't want any slip-ups or missing evidence, do we?" He smirked before going back to his office.

Stagg noticed Wilkins stiffen in response to Burns' comments, and he wasn't surprised when Wilkins muttered, "Blinking cheek!" under his breath.

"Okay, Wilkins?"

"Sir!" Wilkins stomped back into the main office and sat beside Hudson.

"Everything all right? Here's some more lists to check for green vehicles." Hudson handed him several long sheaves of paper.

"Thanks! Don't you get fed up with doing these checks? It's not very demanding police work, is it?"

"No, but sometimes one detail can change a whole case, so it's still important."

"Yes, but I should be out there, interviewing suspects and criminals, not sat in here, looking at boring registration numbers! I came top in the observation studies in police training, you know."

"Really? Well, you should be able to pick through these lists in a jiffy, shouldn't you?"

"No, I've got an idea. I'm just going to check something out."

"But where are you going?"

"To the gipsy camp, of course! It's what Inspector Burns suggested. I won't be long if you can inform Inspector Stagg." Before Hudson could say anymore, Wilkins had left.

Wilkins whistled as he drove through town in a cheerful mood. If his hunch were correct, he'd find a green Cortina at the gipsy camp, which would solve the case. It would be a good start, and his uncle would be pleased. Stagg was thorough, but Wilkins thought he was a bit slow. He was going to be much faster in his investigations.

Wilkins arrived at the camp, where a fire was burning in its midst. The wooden caravans were sited in a semi-circle, and the two modern vans were near the entrance. A green Cortina was parked up, but it had a wheel missing and was propped up in a rough fashion with wooden blocks and rocks.

A man in trousers and a vest approached Wilkins. "Everything all right? What are you snooping round here for?" He didn't seem very friendly. Wilkins stood up straight and flashed his police badge to the surly man.

"I'm from the police, and I believe this vehicle has been involved in a robbery. Who's the owner?"

"I am, and I don't know what you're talking about! I haven't done any robbery! Why would I? I'm rich, aren't I?" The man laughed but picked up a stout walking stick. "Now, if you don't mind, get away from my car! Maybe it was a mistake to come here on your own!"

"Never mind that! Now, where were you last Friday? And don't lie to me, my lad!"

Wilkins quickly stepped away from the man and walked around to where the car was propped up. He squatted down and peered underneath, pretending to know what he was looking at. The car wobbled a little, and there was a sudden creak. Wilkins felt his overcoat collar tighten as he was roughly pulled out of harm's way before the car crashed to the floor at his side. Wilkins was hurled to the ground. He jumped up and was confronted by Stagg's angry face.

"Wilkins! What are you doing here?"

"Sir! I thought I'd find the green Cortina, sir. And I have. Look!"

"You've found a Cortina, Wilkins."

"But sir! See!" Wilkins insisted as he pointed.

"I told him I don't know anything about a robbery, but he didn't listen. So, I thought I'd scare him a bit," the man in the vest said.

"Indeed! Come on, Wilkins."

Ralph, the gipsy elder in the black hat, approached. "Stagg! Hello. No trouble, is there?" He glared at Wilkins, who was brushing himself down.

Stagg shook his head. "Hello, Ralph. How are you? No trouble. Just someone getting the wrong end of the stick. See you again, Ralph."

Wilkins said, "But sir! How do you know that car isn't the one?"

Stagg stopped. "If you'd looked carefully, you'd have noticed that there were no tyre tracks in front of the car at all, and it's a bit of a muddy site. It doesn't do to make unfounded accusations, Wilkins."

"But, sir. They're gipsies! They always cause trouble. Don't they?"

Ralph put his arm out to stop the man in the vest from springing forward. "Don't, Leo! He doesn't know what he's saying. A trainee, is he, Stagg?"

"Something like that, Ralph. Sorry to trouble you. Come on, Wilkins!"

"But, sir...." Stagg stopped and glared at Wilkins.

"If it's one thing you need to learn, Wilkins, it's this. Never, ever make assumptions about anyone. I would have thought that was the first thing they'd have taught you in training. You should never judge anyone by where they're born or where they live!"

"Yes, sir. Sorry, sir."

"Lesson learnt, Wilkins? Good! Let's get back to those checks, shall we?" Stagg pushed Wilkins gently towards his car, and watched Wilkins drive off, then nodded to Ralph before leaving.

CHAPTER 6

The next day, at the station, Stagg's phone rang. "Stagg here."

"Sir? It's PC Jones. Sergeant Roberts asked me to tell you there's been another robbery. At Blackheath, sir. Jewellery this time, a lot of it. They've coshed the shopkeeper. It's Williams Jewellers, on High Street."

"I know it. Thanks, Jones. I'll be there in ten minutes!"

Stagg sped into the main office, where Wilkins was poring over a long printout while Hudson checked another. "Wilkins! Come on!"

"Sir?" Wilkins jumped up, knocking some sheets of paper off the desk. "Sorry," he smiled sheepishly to Hudson.

"Wilkins! Come on! You want to do real police work, don't you?" Stagg strode out of the room, with Wilkins running after him, trying to put his coat on at the same time. Hudson picked up the papers and smiled.

***

At Blackheath, Stagg pulled up in front of Williams Jewellers. There was no sign of any damage to the shop's exterior, and the policeman outside was the only indication that anything out of order had happened. Three or four people milled about, curious.

As Stagg got out of his car, an elderly lady pulling a shopping trolley behind her asked him, "Are you in charge here?" Wilkins stepped in front of Stagg.

"Now come along. The inspector can't talk to you now, madam." He stood with his back to the woman. Stagg glared at Wilkins, walked around him and approached the lady.

"Yes, I'm Inspector Stagg. I'm just going into the shop. Can I help you?"

"Only I saw them, you know. I saw what happened. There were two of them. Yes, a big one and a thin, weedy chap. You know, shifty looking."

"I see. Do you remember anything else, such as their car?"

"Course I remember!" The lady huffed, drawing herself up to her full height of five feet. "It was a red one, a red Cortina. I know it was a Cortina because my grandson's got one just like it. Oh! Not that it was him, of course. He's got a good job at the Baines factory up the road."

"You've been very helpful, madam." Stagg motioned to the policeman at the door. "This lady would like to tell you what she saw, Roberts."

"Sir!" The policeman pulled out his notebook.

"Thank you very much indeed. We'll be in touch if we need any more help," said Stagg as he stepped up to the door to where Wilkins was waiting. "Not gone in yet? I thought you'd have solved the case by now!" Stagg opened the door with a steely look in his eye.

Two women were in the shop. The thin one sitting on a chair dabbed her eyes with a white lace handkerchief while a younger one leaned against a glass display case nearby. A few black velvet trays were askew on one of the counters. They both looked up when the two men came inside.

"Hello. I'm Inspector Stagg. How are you both? Been a big shock for you, I expect?"

"Oh, yes, Inspector," the thin woman squeaked. "Poor Mr Williams! They were so awful, weren't they, Betty?"

The young woman whispered, "Yes, they were." She was pale and gripped her fingers tightly in her lap.

"Do you mind waiting here while I ask Mr Williams some questions? And don't touch anything, please. Thank you. Is Mr Williams through here" Stagg pointed to the back of the shop. The tall sales assistant nodded.

"All right, we won't. I'm Miss Ellis, by the way," she whispered to Stagg. "Mr Williams is just resting in the back. Actually, he shouldn't be in at all, you know." Stagg caught a whiff of Lily of the Valley perfume—his Nan used to wear it.

"I'll just go through then. Wilkins, you stay here with the ladies." He paused in the doorway and called through. "Hello, Mr Williams. I hope you don't mind my calling to see you if you have a moment."

A small balding man looked up. He had some bad bruising on his cheek and on top of his head. He also had a plaster over his nose, and it looked as if he was developing two black eyes. He looked quite forlorn.

"This is the police, Mr Williams, and they'd like a word, if you don't mind," Betty said.

"Yes, Betty. No, I don't mind at all. Come in. I just want you to catch whoever did this and get my jewellery back." Betty hovered near the doorway. "Don't come in here now, Betty, please. I'm having a quiet word with the policeman."

"Sorry, Mr Williams." Betty went back into the shop and stood by Miss Ellis and Wilkins. Stagg motioned Wilkins to come across to the back office.

"Sir?"

"Could you ask Miss Ellis to show you the area near the window locks, Wilkins? That is all right, isn't it, Mr Williams?"

"Well, if you must. But please be careful. I've not much stock as it is!" He dabbed his head.

"Yes, Mr Williams. We'll be very careful not to touch anything until they've dusted for fingerprints, won't we, Wilkins?"

"Yes, sir."

"Now, if we can just recap. I know it's upsetting for you, Mr Williams, but can you tell me exactly what you remember from the robbery, sir?"

"Yes, I can. And I'm not upset, just angry. I want you to catch those men and get my rings back, and that's all!" He winced and put his hand to his head again.

"Of course, sir. Are you all right? Yes?" The man nodded. "All right then. Now, take your time and tell me what happened."

"We were just going to change the stock around. We do it once a week, so it looks like we've got plenty of stock." Mr Williams blew his nose. "We'd changed one set of rings around and were just doing the second lot when he marched in. He had a stocking on his head and a cap, and he took a crowbar out of his work bag."

"He? I thought there were two?"

"One, at first. The other one burst in after him, from nowhere, it seemed like."

"I see. Did you notice anything about them, sir? Anything at all?"

"Well, to be honest, it was a bit funny. It was what he was wearing on his feet! The one with the crowbar wore a pair of brown boots. Huge they were! He was the one who pushed me around, and I fell. Once I'd opened my safe and the window locks, they told us to get in the back room here. Then after they'd got what they wanted, they told us all to keep quiet. But I tried to grab my jewels, and that's when the big chap hit me. He hit me a couple of times, I think." The old man's shoulders shuddered at the memory of his assault.

"Anything else you noticed, sir? Sorry, I know it's upsetting for you."

"No, not really. Oh, the other chap wore a pair of white plimsolls. You know, like running shoes."

"I see. Can you give me a description of the men?"

"The first one to come in was quite big. Stocky chap with fair hair, I think. It was hard to see under the stocking. He was wearing a dark cap, but that slipped off when I tried to grab my stock. The other was thin and dark, not someone you'd really notice, if you know what I mean." He mopped his head again. Stagg got up and got him a drink of water.

"Here we are. Take your time, sir." Stagg waited a couple of minutes, noting the small sink, shelving and a black safe tucked away in the corner, which now stood open. There was a table and two chairs, and an outside door and a long silk curtain was swept back across the doorway. The frail man sipped at the water. "Okay if I proceed?" Stagg leant forward.

"Yes, sorry. It's all been a bit too much. I don't want to go home. My wife fusses so much, you see."

"I understand, sir."

"Ah! So, you're married too, are you? They do fuss, women, don't they?" said the little man.

"Me? No, sir. I never got around to it somehow, but I'm sure they mean well. Now, where does this back door lead to? May I have a look?"

"Yes. It's only a yard but do look at it, if you wish. I'll stay here. You can take my keys." He handed Stagg a ring full of keys of all sizes. "Here, it's this one for the door."

"Yes, that's fine, you rest there. I won't be a moment, sir."

Stagg preferred to take a look on his own. The door was unlocked, and he stepped out. The yard was a few feet wide and housed a steel bin, a brush, a mop bucket and a mop. He walked over to the wooden gate, which was bolted. Stagg unlocked it and saw that it gave way to a narrow alley. He closed, bolted and locked it again, reached into his pocket for a handkerchief, wiped his hands and went back into the shop.

"Is everything all right?" asked Mr Williams.

"Yes. Where does the alley lead to?"

"It leads to the end of the street. We only use it when the dustmen come to collect the bins."

"And what day is that?"

"Tuesdays."

"And you lock the gate each time?"

"Oh, yes. We like to be secure, for obvious reasons." The little man stood up.

"Yes, of course. I just wondered, that's all. Thank you, Mr Williams. You've been very helpful. Oh, just one more thing, sir. The ladies who work here, do they live locally?"

"Yes, both of them do. Miss Ellis lives in Park Avenue, and Betty lives in Garden Village, er, Hawthorn Drive, I think, one of the council houses. Both are respectable women and are trustworthy."

"I see. Well, thank you again."

Stagg went back into the main shop. Betty was giggling at something that Wilkins was saying. Miss Ellis held a duster in her hand, keen to tidy up, but she knew she couldn't until the place had been dusted for fingerprints.

She had been watching Inspector Stagg from behind one of the glass display cases and was thankful for the gentle way he had questioned poor Mr Williams. He had had a terrible shock after all! She compared the inspector to his young companion, who was chatting to Betty in a very easy-going manner, not like a policeman should be chatting at all! No, there was a lot to be said for old-fashioned respect, and Inspector Stagg certainly showed that.

"Could we ask you both a few questions, ladies?" Stagg asked.

"No, we don't mind, sir. We will help you all we can, won't we, Betty?" Miss Ellis carefully folded up her hanky and tucked it up her sleeve.

Stagg nodded at Wilkins. "If you have a chat with Betty, Wilkins?" He turned to Miss Ellis. "And your full name is?"

"My name is Miss Anne Ellis. I've worked here for fifteen years, and I'm the senior sales assistant. We've never had any trouble like this before in all the time I've worked here. My goodness, no!" She spoke, gasping at the air in snatches. Her eyes welled up again, and out came her hanky. She wiped them delicately. Stagg smiled.

"I'm sure, Miss Ellis. Now, where were you when these people entered the shop?"

"Ah, I was in the shop, by the window, near Mr Williams, the proprietor." She gulped. "We were just going to change the rings around, you see. We do it once a week. It's good to move the stock around, and it gives the impression that we have more stock than we actually have. We'd only just unlocked the windows when he came in."

"Unlocked the windows?"

"Yes, sir, I'll show you." She got up quickly.

"Not just yet, Miss Ellis. Don't touch anything, please." Miss Ellis nodded and sat down again, smoothing her black pencil skirt.

"Yes, of course, sir."

She looked at the inspector who was standing before her. He must be about six feet tall. She noted his greying temples, but it was his eyes that made his face so compelling. She was sure they had scrutinized everything in the small shop, including herself. She pointed to the panelled doors at the back of the window displays.

"Of course, these are normally kept locked during the day."

"I see," said Stagg. He turned when he heard laughter coming from Betty, who was speaking to Wilkins. "Now, Betty, where were you when all this happened?"

The girl's eyes widened. "Me? Oh, I was just telling your assistant. I was in the back, making the tea. We always have tea at three o'clock, don't we, Miss Ellis?"

"Yes, we do, actually."

"Did you see or hear anything, Betty?" asked Stagg.

"No. Only a lot of shouting, like I just told him." She nodded to Wilkins and twisted her blonde hair with her fingers. "I was in the back. I was too frightened to come out at first."

"So, you did come out?"

"Well, yes. One chap was shouting at Mr Williams. He wanted him to show him the safe and open it. Then another one appeared, and they both came into the back room, so I came out then. But Mr Williams wouldn't open it. He just wouldn't! And they hit him!" Her voice turned to a whisper again, and she looked down. "They hit him a few times. They shouldn't have done that. They shouldn't. It was awful!"

"I see. Did they tell you to get out of the room?"

"No. Why would they do that? Why would they speak to me?" she sniffed. Stagg gave her a cool assessing glance, and Betty looked away.

"Right, Wilkins. Miss Ellis, here are the chaps to do the fingerprints. Once they've finished, you can have a bit of a tidy."

"Thank you, sir," said Miss Ellis. "Actually, we can't do much here as it is today. If you've finished questioning, Inspector, maybe Betty can go home. I'll hang on a while." Miss Ellis tried a brief smile and brought up her chin in a determined fashion.

"Wilkins? Have you taken Betty's statement?" Wilkins nodded, scribbling in his notebook. "That's fine, then," Stagg said.

The young girl grabbed her bag and coat. "Bye!" she shouted.

Stagg nodded to Betty as she left the shop. "She doesn't hang about, does she? How long has she been working here?" he asked Miss Ellis.

"About three months. She's a lovely girl with very good references."

"I see. And what was on these black trays, Miss Ellis?"

"Why, rings, of course. Mostly solitaires, actually, and some clusters."

"Clusters?" asked Wilkins, who had greeted the forensics team. of diamonds, young man!" Miss Ellis sniffed at him and nodded to Inspector Stagg.

"Well, goodbye. It's been very upsetting for you all but don't worry about Mr Williams, Miss Ellis. I'm sure he'll be fine in a day or two," Stagg said quietly.

"Goodbye, sir," said Miss Ellis. *'What a kind, charming man Inspector Stagg was,'* she thought, *'especially for a policeman.'*

As soon as they got into the car, Wilkins blurted, "Well, sir? Did you find anything out?"

"I was just about to ask you the same question, Wilkins." Stagg drove off and noticed that the young officer's cheeks had turned pink.

"Oh, not much, I'm afraid. We were talking about the local pubs, actually. But I did ask her if she noticed anything unusual about the robbers. She hadn't, only that one of them was tall, large with red hair! She mentioned that a couple of times and made a bit of a joke about it. After all, who would do a robbery if they had bright red hair?" Wilkins chuckled.

"Did you advise her that you were noting all this down? You got her full name and address, I take it?"

"Yes, I did, sir. She joked about that too, asking if she was the chief suspect or something." Wilkins' cheeks were quite flushed now.

"I don't suppose she mentioned anything about shoes to you?"

"Shoes? Why would she mention shoes?" Wilkins sneered, then saw Stagg's eyebrows arch. "Sorry sir, no, she didn't mention shoes."

"And Miss Ellis? Did she say anything to you?"

"Oh, nothing much. She was too busy watching all the time. She muttered something when you went outside in the back, though."

"Oh, what was that?"

"Something about the gate, I didn't really catch. Sorry, sir."

"In future, you need to take more notes and pay attention. You're not a new constable, Wilkins!"

"No, sir. I just thought…."

"No room for thought, Wilkins. You have to follow procedure, or else you'll be butchered in a court of law. Bear that in mind in the future."

"Yes, sir. Sir, is that what Burns meant about missing evidence?"

"What? Oh, that was something that happened a long time ago, Wilkins. None of your concern."

Stagg drove on for a couple of miles, thinking back to when he was a desk sergeant. Burns had pulled in a couple of crooks on a charge, and as per procedure, Stagg had got them to empty their pockets. Amongst the items was a black notebook, in which were listed names and addresses. Stagg had placed it in an envelope on the station desk before escorting the crooks to their cells. When he'd returned, the notebook had gone missing, and Burns didn't let Stagg forget it.

Stagg drove on. "Which pub did that girl in the shop say she goes to, then? It might be worth checking."

"The White Lion, sir, on Salop Road."

"I know it."

"But why do you want to go there?"

"Explore all avenues, that's my motto. You never know where they may lead."

He pulled into the station yard and barked, "Make a few notes on what the girl said if you can remember and leave your report on my desk."

"Yes, sir."

Stagg thought about the employees at Williams Jewellers, particularly Betty. She seemed really upset, or was she just shocked by the robbery? After completing his reports on the jewellery robbery and satisfying himself that he had done enough investigation work for one day, Stagg went home.

It was a fine evening, and he mulled over the day's events while he pushed his lawnmower along. This would be the last cut of the year. He picked up a small pebble off the lawn and threw it into the borders that were full of rose bushes.

He reached down to empty the grass box. One of his neighbours shouted, "Cutting your grass again, Mr Stagg? You can do mine after yours if you like!"

"Ha, yes! I've got enough to do with my own, thanks," he chuckled.

After checking the borders for weeds, he surveyed his front garden. He'd already manured the roses for over the winter. He still couldn’t seem to grow roses as well as his grandad, however hard he tried. But he had to admit they had put on a pretty good display this year, especially the pink ones.

Stagg remembered how he had once taken a bunch for Hazel as a surprise when she’d called off their date because she didn’t feel very well. As he’d approached her house, he’d watched her run out and jump into a car—Burns’ car. That was a long time ago. The pain he'd felt had dulled to almost nothing now, and working with the perpetrator made things worse. It was fortunate for Inspector Burns that Stagg behaved professionally.

CHAPTER 7

The next day, Stagg had just sat down at his desk when the chief rang him.

"Stagg? Well? How are you getting on with the jewellery job? Any leads? Anything on the Baines robbery?" he snapped.

"We're doing the routine checks, sir. I…."

"Well, you'd better get a move on! Now you've got extra help, I'm expecting you to crack these robberies. You should have something by now, Stagg! Get to it!" He rang off.

"Yes, bloody sir!" Stagg muttered, making a mock salute at the phone just as Hudson passed the door. She looked down, but he was sure she was smiling. Where was that Wilkins anyway? Stagg looked through some paperwork. There were reports of a bike theft, somebody shoplifting, and a car driving off without paying for petrol—all run-of-the-mill stuff. Hudson tapped his door.

"Sir? Wilkins said he'll be delayed today. He's had to take his mother to a hospital appointment." Stagg glanced at the reports on his desk.

"What? Right, okay, Hudson, thanks."

Wilkins marched into the police station an hour later. Stagg rolled his eyes. *'You'd think Wilkins owned the place!'* Stagg thought. He wondered how important Wilkins would feel now that he had to write up an actual report. Stagg returned to his office, passing a blonde WPC on the way. She smiled at him, but he didn't see her. Stagg called Wilkins into his office and closed the door.

"Wilkins, I understand you were late coming in this morning?"

"Yes, sir. I had to take my mother to an appointment."

"Couldn't someone else have taken her? Or could she have got a taxi?"

"A taxi? I was only half an hour late, sir, and it's not as if I was busy. I was only supposed to be doing those car checks with Hudson. It's pretty boring, if you ask me!"

"I see." Stagg drummed his fingers on the desk. "How long have you wanted to become a police officer, Wilkins?"

"What? Oh, well, I don't know, really. Mother thought it might be a good career for me, and with my Uncle Brian being the chief, well, it seemed a pretty easy route to follow. He helped me to become a police trainee, but I passed all my exams myself. He didn't help me with those, sir."

"I should hope not! Now, listen, Wilkins! As my assistant, you can't just stroll in here whenever you like, and you can't do what you like. Checking through information, which includes lists, is an important part of the job. I expect you to do any task I ask of you, irrespective of your uncle being the chief inspector! Use your initiative by all means but follow my orders! Is that understood?"

"Yes, sir!"

"Good! Dismissed!"

After a few minutes, Hudson popped her head around the door. "Fancy a cup of tea, sir? I'm just making one."

"Great! Just what I need. Thanks." A couple of minutes later, she put a mug of tea on his desk, along with some ginger biscuits. "I am honoured. Biscuits as well, Hudson." He smiled and flashed his steely eyes on her. Then he looked down, and after sipping his tea, he asked, "Do you get into town much, Hudson, on your nights off?"

"Town, sir?" She flushed a little and cleared her throat. "Sometimes, sir."

"Ever go to The White Lion on Salop Road?"

"I've been there once, sir, yes. It gets busy there on the weekend." She clasped her hands tightly around her back.

"I want you to go there this Saturday." Stagg noticed her pink cheeks. He looked down at some papers on his desk. "It's a bit of undercover work, Hudson. I want you to see if the girl from the jewellers will be there, and more importantly, who she's with. I'll wait in the car outside. I don't want her to see me. I can show you who she is later today, if you like."

Stagg knew what she had been thinking and felt angry. He just didn't want to disappoint anyone, especially Hudson. She was a nice girl. The WPC looked down.

"That's okay, sir. I can call into the jewellers myself. Oh, that's my phone. Sorry, sir!" She darted back to her desk.

Stagg sighed, slammed his desk drawer shut and got up from his chair. Wanting to visit the Baines factory again, he decided to leave Wilkins on the car checks with Hudson.

***

When Stagg arrived at the Baines factory gates, a few men were chatting outside. Stagg nodded to one of them.

"Hello, there. I'm Inspector Stagg. I don't suppose any of you were still here last Friday night, were you? I'm just checking some things out."

One man replied, "No, none of us were here. We all finish early on a Friday, at half past four, don't we, lads?" The other men nodded in agreement.

"And you didn't see anything out of the ordinary when you left?"

"No, sorry."

"Is Mr Baines a good employer?"

"What do you mean?"

"Well, is he strict, watching working times, for example?"

"He checks we arrive and leave on time. I'm shop steward here, and we haven't had any disputes or anything, if that's what you mean. He's like any boss, isn't he, lads? And we'd better get inside, or he'll finish us and all!"

"Oh? Has he sacked anyone recently?"

"No, he didn't sack them. Made them redundant. They were older blokes."

"What about the new contract?"

"New contract? We don't know anything about a new contract. Sorry, I must go in!"

"Yes. Thank you."

Stagg walked back to his car. When he got back to the station, he phoned Mr Baines.

"Hello, Mr Baines. It's Inspector Stagg here. I'm sorry to trouble you, but you mentioned you were going to visit Birmingham regarding a new contract. Who was that with, please? Just for the record."

"What's that got to do with anything, Stagg? Nothing at all, I suppose!"

"If you'd humour me, sir."

"I don't see what difference it makes. Johnson's Electricals, if you must know. Goodbye!"

Stagg contacted Johnson's. They knew nothing about a new contract with Baines unless he was just ordering 'on spec'. Stagg noted it down, and he needed to chat with the store's person at the Baines factory.

He dialled the number for the Baines factory and asked for the stores. The switchboard operator didn't ask for his name, so Stagg didn't reveal it. He was put straight through to stores.

"Hello, I've just got a quick enquiry, sir, if you don't mind?" asked Stagg.

"Oh! Yes, I see. What can I do for you?"

"I understand that Mr Baines was going to place an order with Johnson's Electricals in Birmingham. Do you know anything about it?"

"Johnsons? Now, why would he do that? We're all stocked up. Who did you say this was?"

"Ah, I see. It doesn't matter. It must be my mistake. Thanks for your help. Goodbye."

Stagg strummed his fingers on his desk. So what exactly was Baines going to do with all the money that had gone missing? Stagg knew he was married. Maybe it was for a personal matter or a special occasion. Maybe he was having an affair.

CHAPTER 8

Ideally, Saturday night could have been special for Hudson. It was raining cats and dogs, and Stagg picked Hudson up at seven-thirty. She rushed into the car, spraying droplets of rain everywhere. She was wearing a short cream Mackintosh with white knee-length boots, and her hair was loose and curled up around her shoulders. Her scent filled the car, and she was smiling.

"Sorry, sir." She wriggled herself into her seat. "Gosh, what a horrible night!"

Surprised at how lovely she looked, Stagg turned away when she got in and drove off once she had closed her door.

"Yes. Now listen carefully, Hudson. This isn't a trip out," Stagg grunted. He was being abrupt, and he hated himself for it.

"Yes, sir. Sorry, sir," she snapped back.

"You've seen the girl? Betty?"

"Yes, sir. I went to the jewellers, so I know who she is. I saw her through the window."

"Good. I want you to see who she's with, if there's anyone in particular, you know."

"A boyfriend?"

"Yes, or anyone she has any long chats with."

"I see. Do you think she's got something to do with the robbery, sir?"

"I don't know, Hudson, maybe." He pulled up across the road from The White Lion.

"Now, I'll wait here. I'll be watching people coming and going."

"But how long will you wait, sir?"

"Till you leave, Hudson."

"But I could be in there all night," Hudson gasped.

"Yes, you could. Oh, that reminds me, here's five pounds so you can have a drink. That should be plenty. Ginger beer, mind. No drinking on duty. Off you go."

Hudson slammed the door shut and ran across the road. She wondered how Stagg had talked her into this and whether Betty would turn up at all. She shook the rain from her hair and went to the bar to get herself a drink. She chose a seat in a quiet corner where she could see people coming and going and loosened her coat.

Stagg waited five minutes, then got out of his car and walked in the opposite direction to the pub and crossed the road. He quickly backtracked and passed the pub, glancing in the window as he did so and could see where Hudson was seated. He went on for a hundred yards, then crossed back over and got back into his car and waited. He liked to know where his officers were positioned.

A man entered the pub at about nine o'clock. He noticed the curvy girl in the white boots sitting on her own. She wasn't a regular and thought he might try his luck later. He bought himself a drink, then watched her while he played snooker with some other regulars.

It was getting late, and Pamela Hudson decided to get one more drink. The pub was starting to fill up now with all sorts. She had to wait a while to be served but managed to get back to her seat. She scanned the room over her glass to see if she could see Betty, but there was no sign. She noticed a man in the corner near the snooker table giving her the eye but took no notice.

Several young couples arrived, along with the usual drunken yobs who'd been on the beer all afternoon at the local working men's club. There were some young chaps who were looking out for fresh talent near the bar and a crowd of young, giggling girls in the opposite corner. Pamela had received quite a few admiring glances, but she ignored these. She was going off the ginger ale now that she'd had two. She decided to get a pineapple juice instead, but it was very busy at the bar, so she waited her turn in the crowd.

"Let me get that for you, darling," a voice said behind her. She turned to see the man who'd been eyeing her up. He had yellow teeth, and his breath stank of stale cigarette smoke.

"No, it's fine, thank you," she said, turning back around to the bar. She felt his body push against her, and she pushed back, turning around.

"Do you mind?"

"Sorry, love, it's packed in here."

"Yes, it is." She edged away from him.

"Aren't you having a drink? I can buy you whatever you like, darling, whatever you want. I've been watching you get the drinks down you. You like your drink, don't you?" His gaze ran over her body. The crowd pushed forward again, and she felt his hand on her bottom. The grip turned into his hands stroking her. She felt sick and needed some air.

"Excuse me!" she shouted and pushed past him.

"In a hurry, aren't you? Next time, maybe." He shrugged his shoulders and turned back to the bar. Getting his glass, the man went back to the snooker table and slowly drank his beer.

Hudson hurried out of the pub into the cold night. She could still smell the man's putrid breath on her face. She was glad of the freshness of the rain, washing it away. She hurried, half walking, half running down the street.

Stagg had seen her exit the pub and knew she was upset as soon as he'd seen her. He waited a couple of minutes, in case she was followed, and then drove down the street. Hudson was still striding onwards, but she jumped in Stagg's car when it pulled up in front of her.

"Are you all right? What happened?"

"Yes, sir. Nothing, sir."

"You're sure?"

"Yes. Just some creep trying it on."

"I see. Well, we'll call it a night. It's getting late. I don't think Betty's coming here tonight."

"No, sir."

Pamela Hudson looked out of the window and felt stupid for feeling so upset. She put on her belt and was glad of the sanctuary of Stagg's car. She rested her head back on the headrest and watched the wipers clean the windscreen as Stagg started the car.

Stagg reflected that it had been a bit mean to have asked her to work on a Saturday night. He said, "Come on. We'll go to the Talbot in Whitmere and have a quiet nightcap. What do you say?"

"No. No, sir. It's all right. Oh, I've got change out of the five pounds, sir."

"Well, you can keep that. That chap, he didn't touch you, did he, Hudson? If I thought that, I would never have asked you…."

"No, sir. He was just creepy. But he didn't touch me. Well, not really."

"Not really?" Stagg braked and looked across at her.

"No! He just pushed himself against me, that's all."

"Oh, did he?" Stagg snarled, surprising himself as much as Hudson. "But you're all right, though, aren't you?"

"Yes, I am. It just wasn't very nice, that's all."

"No, I'm sorry. I shouldn't have asked you, Hudson. It was a stupid idea."

"It's okay, sir, really." Stagg didn't know what to say, so he drove on for a few minutes.

"So, what do you do on a Saturday night? Normally, I mean."

Hudson sighed. "Not that much, sir. Sometimes I go out with friends."

"Oh, of course. Sorry, I didn't ask if you had plans with your boyfriend."

"I didn't, sir. I don't have one at the moment." She didn't want to sound desperate.

"I see. Well, I normally have fish and chips on a Saturday night."

"Do you?" Hudson smiled, relaxing a little.

"Well, not every Saturday. Do you fancy some tonight? We'll just make the one on Strange Street if we're quick." Stagg felt it was the least he could do as he felt awful that Hudson had been upset.

"Okay, sir. Why not? Only can I be cheeky and ask for potato scallops? You know, potato pieces in batter? I prefer them to chips."

"Scallops it is, Hudson."

Stagg drove to the local chip shop, then went to a lay-by near the lake on the other side of town. He had forgotten that it was a popular place for courting couples and had come here once or twice with Hazel. Hudson didn't seem bothered by his choice, and he was relieved to see no other cars there. It was still relatively early.

"Thanks for tonight, Hudson. I do appreciate it." He ate some of his chips. "Hmm, I don't suppose you'd do the same again next Saturday, would you? That Betty's bound to turn up there soon."

"Yes, okay, sir. That should be all right." Hudson finished eating her fish and potato scallops. The battered slices were delicious. She stretched. "Ooh, a lie-in in the morning. Smashing! Are you doing anything nice, sir?"

"Me? Oh, the usual, you know."

"No, I don't."

"Don't what?"

"Don't know what the usual is."

"Oh, sorry. Well, I read the Sunday papers and do a bit of gardening. Usual things a chap does on a Sunday."

"I see."

"And? What do you do on a Sunday, Miss Hudson?"

"The usual," they both said at the same time and laughed. Stagg noticed a feeling starting to grow inside him—it must be the chips.

"No, sir, I sometimes go for a bike ride. Do a bit of hand washing, have a bath and then do some ironing for work on Monday. That's it. Bit boring, really." She laughed, and Stagg smiled.

They finished their supper, enjoying the view of the lake, dappled with silvery lights from the rain. In different circumstances, it was quite a romantic spot. They both scrunched up the chip papers and when another car parked nearby, Stagg decided it was time to go.

"Well, I suppose we'd better get back." He started the car and drove her home. He waited for her to get to her front door and waved as he drove away. Stagg smiled. It had been a good evening all round. He'd seen a car drop someone off at The White Lion, but the driving rain prevented him from seeing the registration plate. He was sure it was a red Cortina.

CHAPTER 9

On Monday morning, Stagg was at his desk early and checked the vehicle reports. No one had been able to give the registration number of the red Cortina. The patrol cars had been alerted to keep a lookout for it while on their rounds.

Stagg decided to phone the jewellers and hopefully have a word with Miss Ellis. She might be able to help. He looked at his watch, and it was eight-thirty. They'd just be opening, so the shop should be quiet.

Wilkins appeared at the door. Stagg motioned him to sit down and dialled the jeweller's number. "I won't be long, Wilkins, so just sit down a minute." He didn't mind the young lad, really. It was just the way the chief had thrust Wilkins upon him.

Miss Ellis answered the phone. "Williams Jewellers. How can I help you?" Stagg introduced himself. "Oh, hello, Inspector. What can I do for you this morning? Do you wish to speak to Mr Williams? Actually, I'm afraid he's just in the back room. I can call him if you like."

"I see. No, I wanted a word with you, Miss Ellis."

"Oh, dear me. What have I done? Nothing wrong, I hope?"

"No, Miss Ellis, nothing wrong. Is Betty Griffiths in today?"

"Yes, she's just arrived. She's in the back at the moment with Mr Williams and looks a bit worse for wear, actually. I think she went out with that sister of hers at the weekend, and they had too much to drink," she whispered.

"Does she do that regularly?"

"Well, about once a month, I would say. You know what these youngsters are like." Miss Ellis gave a shrill chuckle.

"Yes, indeed. And her sister lives locally?" Stagg leaned forward in his chair.

"Well, I'm not one to gossip, Inspector, of course," she whispered. "But her sister lives in a big house on that new estate near the golf course. Is it called The Links or something? Her husband must have a good job because Betty's sister isn't very well educated, if you know what I mean. They didn't go to Whytfield Grammar School like I did. Now, what were you going to ask me?"

"Oh, just, if you had remembered anything else about the robbery, anything at all."

"No. I don't think so. No, I've told you everything, I think. Sorry."

"How's Mr Williams?"

"He's getting better, thank you. Actually, we were having a bit of a chuckle before you called. Betty offered to make us a cup of tea, probably because she feels a bit rough. We said as long as it wasn't like the last time."

"Oh?"

"Why, yes, it was the day of the robbery. We take it in turns, you see. Betty always takes her time making the tea. Let's hope she's a bit quicker today."

"Well, thank you, Miss Ellis. Goodbye."

"Goodbye. And remember, if I can be of any service, Inspector, you only have to call."

"Yes, Miss Ellis. Thank you."

Wilkins fidgeted in the chair, spinning a pencil around in his fingers. "Well, sir?"

"Right, Wilkins. Let's have another look at the facts, shall we?"

Wilkins put the pencil on the desk. Stagg went over the witness reports and jotted some notes on a sheet of paper: Brown boots large, white plimsoles medium, big chap with fair or red hair, small weedy sort of chap, a red Cortina.

"What do you think of Betty Griffiths, Wilkins?" The young man flushed a little.

"Betty at the jewellers, do you mean, sir? She seems nice enough."

"I don't mean in that way! What sort of character do you think she is?"

"Sort of character, sir?"

"Yes, character. Did you not study this in your training? Did she strike you as honest, devious, or what?"

"Nothing out of the ordinary, sir. A young girl who tries to act a lot older than she is, if you know what I mean."

"Was she flirting with you then?"

"Not really, sir. Maybe a little. It was funny, really. At first, she seemed upset by the robbery, but then she kept saying that at least no one was seriously hurt."

"Miss Ellis was very upset. What did Betty say about that?"

"Well, she called her a *"daft old thing"*. I asked her if she thought the robbers would return."

"Did you? What did she say?"

"She asked why they would do that and said it had been an awful shock for her."

"Shock?"

"Yes, she said again she couldn't believe it when they hit Mr Williams. That's all I can remember, sir."

"I see. Anything else, Wilkins? This is why it's essential to take notes. How are you getting on with those car checks?"

Wilkins rolled his eyes. "Okay, sir, but I don't have to do those again, do I?"

"All routine checks can be important. I'm sure Hudson will be glad of some help."

"She's a bit stern, sir."

"Who? Hudson? You've got to be joking!" Stagg flicked through the witness statements. "Hold on a minute. Who's this Edna Morris, Wilkins?"

"Oh, she was the old dear with the shopping trolley, sir. You know, the lady who was in your way at the shop, that's all," Wilkins huffed.

"Ah, yes, I remember. All witnesses are important, Wilkins. Let's have a look at what she said." Stagg read the report and passed it over to Wilkins. "So, what do you think? Should we pay Mrs Morris a visit?" Wilkins scanned the report, then handed it back, shrugging his shoulders. Stagg put the report in his drawer and stood up.

"Do you think it's worth a visit, sir? I've still got those checks to do." Wilkins remained seated.

"You can do those later. Come on. We'll go and see what Mrs Morris has to say."

Stagg drove to the council estate and stopped near some pensioners' bungalows. He scanned along the row for number four and strode up the path. When he gently knocked on the door, he saw the lace curtain twitch. Mrs Morris, wearing an apron, opened it.

"Oh, it's you. I've been wondering when you'd decide to visit. Well, come in then." They were shown into a tiny lounge and sat on a settee. Stagg refused a drink, so Mrs Morris sat down.

"These are nice bungalows, Mrs Morris. And it's a quiet area."

"Yes, it's nice and peaceful and not too far from the shops." Mrs Morris nodded.

"Do you ever get any trouble here of any sort?"

"Not really, no. Well, you'd know if there had been, wouldn't you?" she chuckled. "No, we get youngsters round near Bonfire Night, collecting pennies for the Guy, and Christmas, singing carols, in a fashion. That's all, really."

"And your windows and doors are secure?"

"Yes, they are. But you haven't come here to talk about my house, have you? Right, away you go then, with your questions." She put her hands on her lap.

"I'd like you to tell me what you saw at the jewellers on the day of the robbery, Mrs Morris."

"Good! I did tell that sergeant of yours all about it, but I don't think he wrote it all down." She glanced at Wilkins and sniffed. "You know what these youngsters are like."

"Yes, well, Mrs Morris, if you could tell me yourself this time," coaxed Stagg, his notebook open.

Mrs Morris told him how she'd been shopping at the greengrocers opposite the jewellers. "I was taking my time picking out a nice cabbage and a cauliflower, checking them for caterpillars. Then, I saw a red car coming down the high street. I noticed it because it was just like our Billy's car."

"Billy? Who's he?" asked Stagg.

"My nephew."

"I see. What happened then?"

"Well, I could see it wasn't his car, so I carried on checking and finally decided on the cauliflower I wanted. You can do a few things with a cauliflower, you see." Wilkins shifted in his chair, and she glanced sharply at him. "Anyway, I saw a big bloke get out of the car, further down the street, by WH Smith's. He was carrying a work bag, you know, like a plumber's holdall, and he had a dark cap on. He waited outside the jewellers for a minute, looked at his watch, and then turned into the doorway. I didn't see him go in, as I wanted some cooking apples, and they're at the back of the shop."

"Did you make an apple pie?" asked Wilkins. Stagg glared at him, but he was surprised when she answered. "Yes, I did, and very nice it was too. It's all gone, I'm afraid, or you could have both had a slice." She smiled.

"That would have been nice. My old girlfriend Hannah used to make nice apple pies," Wilkins said quietly and looked down. Stagg leant forward in the small armchair.

"Did you see anything else, Mrs Morris?" asked Stagg.

"Yes, when I came out of the greengrocer's, they were just jumping in their car, and they drove off, quick sharp."

"If I could just backtrack a bit. So, you saw one at the door of the shop? Did you see anyone else go in?"

"No, bit funny, really. I only saw that one who waited outside. I'd noticed him because he reminded me of a lad I was in school with years ago—Roger Jones. He was a bit thick and big and a bully but had no brains. I think he must have been waiting for the other one who'd nipped off somewhere."

"Did you see where he'd gone?"

"No, anyway, I saw him look at his watch in the jeweller's doorway. Then later, I saw the two of them coming out. The big one fiddled with something on his head."

"I see. Did you say that the other chap was small then?"

"Not so much small, but he was very thin. I wouldn't trust him. Reminded me a bit of a weasel."

Wilkins shifted in his seat. "A weasel?" he chuckled. Mrs Morris and Stagg ignored him.

"What happened then?" asked Stagg.

"You know what happened! They must have pinched the jewels!"

"No, no. I meant, what did you actually see, Mrs Morris?"

"It was like I said. The shop door was flung open, and the two men came out, half running. Then that thin, snooty woman who works in the jewellers came out, screaming. Lots of people gathered round her. I picked up an orange that someone had knocked off the green grocer's display. People can be so inconsiderate nowadays, can't they?"

Stagg smiled. "Yes, indeed. Now you were saying what happened after you put the orange back, Mrs Morris."

"I'm glad you take notice of what I say. I put the orange back and glanced down the road. Of course, everyone was looking at that woman from the shop. I saw the big chap bolt out first, and then he jumped into the car and started it. The little chap followed him, stuffing things in a black bag. Cheeky blighter when I think of it because he walked to the car. No running for him! Then they drove off, down the road." She sat back in her chair and smiled at the inspector. "And there we are. That's what I saw."

Stagg smiled back at her. "Good. Anything else?"

"Yes, Inspector, there is."

***

The two policemen left the bungalow and walked back to the car.

"Well, who'd have thought it?" said Wilkins, fastening his belt. "She knew the registration number of the robbers' car all the time! Why didn't she tell us before now?"

"Because no one had asked her."

When they returned to the station, Stagg gave Hudson the registration number. "If you could trace the owner for me as soon as you can, please, Hudson," Stagg smiled at her.

"Certainly, sir! I won't be long," she said brightly.

Stagg and Wilkins went into Stagg's office and looked through their notes over a cup of tea. It had been a good afternoon's work. Mrs Morris agreed to make a formal statement at the station the following day and participate in an identification parade. Stagg hoped this would be enough to put the robbers away for some time. Aggravated robbery was a serious matter. It was pure luck that Mr Williams hadn't been seriously hurt.

After a few minutes, Hudson appeared at the door. "Got it, sir. It's registered to a Robert Brooks. Here's the address, sir." She smiled and gave him a sheet of paper but hesitated by the door. "Funny thing is, though, it's down as a green Cortina, not a red one."

"Thanks, Hudson. That's great. Well! Bobby Brooks! Who'd have thought it?"

Wilkins smiled. "Do you know him, sir?"

"Yes, small-time crook. There are two brothers, I think. Yes, that's right. Dad was a bit of a villain—in and out of jail. He's probably dead by now."

Wilkins said, "I know, sir, we're going out again."

"No, not today, Wilkins. I want to make sure Mrs Morris is all right. We need her statement, but we also don't want her to be intimidated by anyone."

"How will they know, sir? We're not going to tell them, are we?"

"Of course not! But Whytfield is a small town, Wilkins, and news seems to travel fast."

"You think they'd frighten her, sir? Really? But she's a lovely old lady."

"I'm glad you think so, Wilkins. Bear in mind that these are villains who don't want to get caught and do time. Believe me, they'll do anything to stop themselves from going inside. No, we'll have to be a bit careful in all this," Stagg mused, and Wilkins nodded his head thoughtfully.

CHAPTER 10

Later that afternoon, Wilkins appeared at Stagg's door. He had been investigating a car that had been involved in an accident the previous week that apparently had no chassis number.

"WPC Jones has found that it was registered to a garage in Whytfield."

"Oh, yes?"

"The garage is over on Whytfield Road. I thought I might pay them a visit, if that's all right, sir."

Stagg looked outside his small office window. It was a dry, bright day. "I'll come with you." He put on his jacket.

Whytfield Motors was a medium-sized garage, with four or five cars parked on the small forecourt. Inside the showroom was a new Rover, newly waxed for a prospective buyer. There was a small desk in the corner of the showroom, and bunches of keys hung from a noticeboard nearby. Jack Evans, the owner, stood up when the two men entered.

"Good afternoon, gentlemen. Can I assist you? We have some very nice cars here for sale, all reasonable prices," he said, nodding constantly. He could see Stagg's blue Wolseley parked outside and wondered if he wanted to trade it in. Stagg nodded at Mr Evans.

Wilkins said, "Good morning. We're police officers, and wondered if you could assist us in tracing a vehicle, please?" He pulled out his police badge and showed it to the man, who had gone quite pale.

"Yes, of course. I'll help, if I can."

Wilkins showed him the registration number and details of the car that had been in the accident, and the man scratched his head. He looked at the note that Wilkins had handed to him again, shaking his head as vigorously as he had been previously nodding it.

"No, no. I don't recall that number. No, I'm sure. I'll check in my book." He stepped over to his desk and got out a diary. Its pages were stained with black, greasy finger-marks, and he flicked through these quickly. He looked up. "No, sorry. There's no matching number in here, and it'd be in the diary. That's where we put all our sales." He put the diary back in the desk drawer.

Wilkins asked, "You're sure? Because it said on our records that it was registered to this garage."

"No, you must be mistaken. I told you, it's not in the book. And if it's not in there, it hasn't been on these premises," the garage owner snapped. Stagg stepped forward and looked down at the seated man.

"Is there any chance, Mr Evans, that someone else could have registered this car to this address, maybe one of your staff?"

"One of my staff? No, they wouldn't do that. They've got more sense!"

"How many people work for you?" Wilkins asked.

"Two. Tony and Barry, both good lads."

"Have they worked for you for long, Mr Evans?" Stagg asked, glad that Wilkins was noting all this down in his notebook.

"Tony's been with me for about ten years, and Barry about three, I think. I'd have to check."

"All right, Mr Evans, not to worry. Would it be possible to have a word with them?"

"Yes, of course. I'll just get them."

They heard him shout beyond a frosted glass door at the back of the showroom. Two men in greasy, navy overalls came through, wiping their hands on their trousers.

"Morning. We were just enquiring if you remember this car from about three months ago." Wilkins showed them the registration number while Stagg watched their expressions. He noticed how the younger man brushed his hand over his head, and he was no longer smiling.

The older mechanic said, "No, I don't remember, sorry."

"I see you've got some paint on your overalls. Do you do paint-spraying here? We're interested in a green Cortina possibly being sprayed red a few months ago for a Mr Bobby Brooks," Wilkins asked.

"Yes, we do, but we haven't done a red Cortina, have we, boys?" Jack Evans asked.

"Oh, Barry did one for a favour for Jan a while back, didn't you? I remember 'cos that red paint gets everywhere." Tony nodded.

"I don't remember that, Tony. What colour was it? Green, you said. No, we haven't had a green car in here, not that I know anyway," said Mr Evans. Tony didn't say any more but just looked at Barry.

"Well, Barry? Do you remember? The car was dark green," Stagg asked. He watched as the young man shook his head and rubbed his hands on his overalls. "You don't remember either vehicle, then? One was registered to this garage. So you're telling me it's a mystery, are you?"

Just then, the showroom door opened, and in walked a fair-headed woman.

"Hello, Jan," Mr Evans started. "This is Jan Brooks. She does the books for me. The police are here, and they're looking for a car." Jan went quite pale and gripped her bag as she walked stiffly over to her desk.

"What car? We have a lot of cars here, don't we?"

Stagg asked, "I'm sure. Now, do you recognise this car registration number? And we'd like to know about Bobby Brooks's car having a paint job. Is he a relation of yours?" Stagg noticed Jan's eyelashes lower so he couldn't see her gaze. She took the paper and stared at it for a few moments.

"No, I don't know that number. Why should I? I wouldn't buy one of those cars. My Charley used to say they were useless."

"Oh, he had one, did he?" Wilkins interrupted.

"Yes. No. No, his friend had one or something, not round here. I don't know. It must have been when he was in Birmingham."

"And Mr Robert Brooks, is he related to you?"

"He might be. I don't have to tell you anything," she snapped.

"You should tell the police, Jan. They'll find out anyway." Jack Evans sat down.

"Okay, he's a distant cousin or something, I don't know. No harm in that, is there? Now, is there anything else? Only I have to get back to my work, you know."

"No, that's all. Thank you."

Mr Evans opened the door as they approached. "I hope we've answered your questions. I don't run a dodgy business here, you know."

"I'm sure you don't, Mr Evans, but that doesn't alter the fact that this vehicle was registered to your garage. We'll be in touch once we've made further enquiries."

"I see. I just don't understand it. I'm trying to build up a good reputation for reliable cars. If this gets out, nobody will want to buy any of my cars!" Jack Evans looked very worried.

"I'm sure there's a simple explanation. Thank you for your help," Stagg said.

Jack Evans regained a bit of his salesmanship. "Nice car you have there, Inspector. I always liked a Wolseley. I had one a few years back, but I traded it in for a Zephyr. If ever you want to sell it, I'd give you a good price." He nodded his head.

"Thanks, but it's not for sale. Goodbye."

Stagg got back into his car. Good price indeed! Wilkins got in beside him.

"I nearly caught that Jan Brooks out then, sir. She's lying, I can tell."

"Yes, I think you might be right. And that chap, Barry. He didn't look very keen to help us either, did he? We'll take another look at the registration logbook, I think. Bit of a coincidence that her name is Brooks, too, isn't it?"

"Yes, I thought that too, sir." Wilkins did seem to be enjoying doing real police work.

***

The following morning, Mrs Morris arrived on time at 10 a.m. to make her statement. Stagg had allowed Wilkins to type up the statement ready, and he had read it back to Mrs Morris. Wilkins asked if she wished to make any adjustments or additions to it.

"No, that's just right, son," Mrs Morris said to Wilkins, and she signed the statement.

Stagg said, "Now you're sure you want to take part in an identification parade once it's set up, Mrs Morris? The people from the jewellers will be there too."

"Yes, yes. That's fine. Anything I can do to help."

"Here's my card if you need to phone me for anything at all," Stagg said.

"Why do I need your card? I've told you everything I know."

"Well, it's just a precaution."

Mrs Morris lifted her head. "Don't you worry about me, Inspector. I've come through two world wars. Two little pipsqueaks aren't going to frighten me, let me tell you!"

"Best to be on the safe side," Stagg said, smiling.

"Yes, you can have my card, too," said Wilkins.

"Oh, you have one too, do you? Well, that's nice that you both care. Well, is there anything else now? I want to pop to the market, you see." She stood up.

"No, that's everything, Mrs Morris." Stagg stood up, towering over the elderly woman. He shook her hand warmly. "Thank you. We'll call you in for the ID parade. It should be in a couple of days."

"Off to the market, did you say? Baking another apple pie?" Wilkins smiled.

"Yes. If you pop round later, you can have some, son. Goodbye now."

"Goodbye," said the policemen in unison.

They both sat down, and Stagg smiled. "Well, I think it's in the bag. Hopefully, the ID parade will prove successful. Then it'll be up in court in a couple of weeks."

"Yes, sir. Erm, if it's okay, sir, could I visit Mrs Morris now and again? It wouldn't be out of order, would it, sir? She reminds me a bit of my grandmother."

"No, that's fine, Wilkins. Now, come on. We'd better get down to organising this ID parade and fast." Stagg got up and followed Wilkins out. He was impressed and surprised at Wilkins' consideration towards Mrs Morris.

"Right, now it's time to pay a visit to our little friends, the Brooks brothers, I think," Stagg said, taking his car keys out of his pocket.

"Great. Let's get at them," Wilkins said.

"Now remember! While I admire your enthusiasm, we have to tread carefully, Wilkins. And definitely no mention of an eyewitness. It's just a routine call to summon them to an ID parade."

"Yes, sir."

Stagg and Wilkins drove to the local council housing estate on the other side of town. Stagg had a rough idea where Bobby Brooks lived as he'd visited the area on various occasions. They turned into a street where the front gardens housed dustbins and long grass. There were no beds of roses here, Stagg noted.

"What's the number of the house?" he asked Wilkins.

"Number five, sir, over there, near the corner." Stagg pulled smartly to the kerb and walked up the path. He knocked on the door gently while Wilkins looked up and down the street. The door was opened by a middle-aged woman wearing a headscarf tied on the top of her head. Two curlers poked out loosely from under the scarf.

"Yes? What is it? I'm not buying anything if you're selling!" She folded her arms, looking at the two men in overcoats. "You're not Mormons, are you?"

"No, we're not, and we're not selling anything. Does a Robert Brooks live here? I'm Inspector Stagg from Whytfield police."

"What if he does? What's it got to do with you?"

Stagg reached into his pocket and pulled out a brown envelope. "I have something for Mr Brooks."

"Do you? I'll see he gets it." The woman snatched the envelope from him.

"It's important that he turns up to his appointment, or he may have to be escorted into the station."

The woman paled. "Escort? Good God! He won't need no escort!" she spat.

"If you could just make sure he has the letter and attends. Thank you."

Stagg and Wilkins returned to the car and drove to the other side of town. He turned into a private estate full of large houses with drives and garages. The gardens here were well-attended, almost manicured. Stagg glanced down at his notebook and pulled the car in front of one of the large houses. The garage door was painted red, which seemed a little incongruous against the others in the street, which were mostly black, white or green.

"Who lives here, sir?" asked Wilkins.

"The other brother, Charley Brooks. Bit different from the other place, isn't it? He's the brains behind most of the schemes they get up to."

"So, you already know about these chaps, sir?"

"Yes, I know their history. Bit of a different job for them this time, if it is them. Aggravated robbery. Nasty!" Stagg glanced out of his car window. "But maybe our Charley needs a bit more money now he's coming up in the world. Come on, let's see who's in."

They went up the path and followed a surprisingly similar scenario to the previous one. This time the door was opened by a very slim woman who wore bright red lipstick and black knee-high boots. She wore too much cheap perfume and had large, gold loops in her ears. It was Jan Brooks. Stagg issued her with a brown envelope.

"What are you doing here? What's this all about? I told you I don't know anything about that car!"

"It's your husband that the summons is for, Mrs Brooks, not yourself," Stagg explained.

"My Charley doesn't get into trouble no more. He's a successful businessman."

"I'm sure he is, so he won't have anything to worry about, will he?" Stagg said. "But he'll need to attend, if you don't mind, or we can send an escort for him."

"Don't you dare send none of your police cars here. This is a respectable area. We're moving up, we are, and I don't want anything spoiled by you lot!" She snatched the envelope from Stagg's hand with her red-painted nails and slammed the door.

"Charming!" Wilkins said as they walked back down the path.

"Indeed!" said Stagg and started up the car.

CHAPTER 11

A couple of days later, Wilkins picked up Mrs Morris, as promised, for the identification parade. Miss Ellis, Betty Griffiths and Mr Williams were picked up by a patrol car. They were all ushered into a small waiting room, where they perched on brown, wooden chairs. Mrs Morris watched Miss Ellis as she pulled nervously on her neck scarf and dabbed her nose delicately with a white handkerchief. No one spoke. Wilkins informed Stagg that the witnesses had arrived.

"Good. Good. Can you tell the sergeant to fetch in the members of the parade, please? Let's get this over and done with." Stagg went to the waiting room and greeted the group. "Good morning! Now, are we all ready? Good. I'll explain the procedure. There will be one parade. They will line up, and they'll be holding cards with numbers on them. All you have to do is note down the ones that you saw on the day of the robbery. You'll be behind a darkened window, so you won't be seen."

"Oh, good, Inspector. I had been so worried about that, actually. You hear of things happening to witnesses, don't you?" Miss Ellis chattered, dabbing her forehead with her handkerchief.

"Don't be daft. This isn't London, you know. They can't see us," Mrs Morris said, sweeping up her handbag. She smiled at Stagg. "Right! Whenever you're ready."

Stagg opened the door and pointed down the corridor. "If you'd follow me, please?"

The witnesses entered a small room with a desk that held several pieces of paper and some brown pencils. Each witness picked one up and sat down on a chair. There was a huge mirror window on one wall, and through this, they could see an outer room with one door. This door suddenly opened, and a group of men walked in and lined up on a line directed by the station sergeant and another police officer.

Stagg's group could see the sergeant directing the men to hold their cards up in front of them but not so high as to hide their faces. They all stared at the dark window, and Stagg noticed Charley Brooks was wearing a smart suit.

"Oh, dear," Miss Ellis whispered. "I can't tell. Is it number three or number five? Oh, and there's a big chap, too, actually." She leant forward, squinting through the glass, but then stepped back quickly as she realised that maybe she could be seen herself.

"What about you, Mr Williams? Do you recognise any of them?" Stagg asked gently.

"No, I can't be certain. They all look so different here. I'm sorry."

"Don't worry, sir. We have plenty of time. Betty? What about you?"

"No, no, I don't know any of them. Nothing to do with me," she stuttered. "I was in the back room, in the shop, remember." She nodded her head.

Stagg said, "Of course you were." He turned to see the old lady sitting on one of the chairs. She was nodding her head.

"Now, Mrs Morris? What about you?"

"Yes. I've noted the number down for you. Here!" She passed him a note.

Betty shouted, "How can you see for sure from the back there?"

"I can see well enough, don't you worry, my girl."

Stagg asked, "Anyone else? Miss Ellis and Mr Williams?"

"No, I'm sorry, Inspector, I can't be a hundred per cent certain," Mr Williams apologised.

"No, I can't either, actually, sir," Miss Ellis added, her handkerchief now a crumpled white ball in her tight fist.

"Very well!" Stagg rang a bell, and the parade filed out. Stagg collected the papers from each one.

"I'd like to thank you all for coming here today. I know it has been a bit nerve-racking for you, and I do appreciate your help. Thank you again." He opened the door and took them to the waiting room. "If you could just wait a few more minutes, thank you."

Stagg summoned Wilkins and another officer to take them home. Once he was sure they were out of the station, he notified the station sergeant. He wanted to make sure that the men in the parade hadn't seen any witnesses.

Stagg returned to his office and got a sheaf of paper to note down the results of the parade. He was a little disappointed that Miss Ellis and Mr Williams didn't fully recognise any of the men but understood that features could be distorted with stockings pulled over them. He jotted down what Betty had said when she was in the room. He'd observed that she'd barely looked at the parade, just giving them a cursory glance.

Stagg pulled out the note that Mrs Morris had given him—number three and number five. That matched up with what Miss Ellis had suggested but hadn't confirmed. He smiled and completed his report.

***

A week later, Wilkins approached Stagg's office and tapped on the doorjamb.

"Sir? I was going to pop across to see Mrs Morris, if that's okay?" Stagg looked up from his paperwork. He'd been surprised that Wilkins was concerned about Mrs Morris, as he remembered how dismissive Wilkins had initially been towards her.

"Yes, of course. I meant to check on her, but you go, by all means, Wilkins."

"Thank you, sir." Wilkins vanished. *'Mrs Morris's apple pie must be good,'* Stagg thought as he sifted through some reports.

The court case for the jewellery job was scheduled for next week, and Stagg was confident of getting the robbers convicted.

He had been double-checking that all the paperwork was in order for a while, when Wilkins returned.

"Is Mrs Morris all right, Wilkins?"

"Yes, sir, she is."

"I've been checking the court papers ready for next week, and I'd like you to check them too, Wilkins. It'll be good practice for you to see how it's to be presented in good order. This is an important case, and I don't want it to be thrown out due to inadequate paperwork." Stagg looked at the young man sternly.

"Yes, sir. You're right, of course. We don't want anything going wrong now."

Wilkins took the reports from Stagg and carefully looked through them. Rain splattered noisily on the window, and red leaves blew down onto the station yard. It was going to be a windy night.

***

The man carefully approached the bungalow. It had been easy to track down the old woman. He'd wanted to warn her off properly, but Charley had said it was too risky and that he should leave it. But he wanted to do something. She deserved it. Then he spotted a ginger cat by her door. He hated cats.

He lured the animal to him with a bit of pork pie, and it miaowed greedily at the stranger. Once it was near enough, the man grabbed it. The cat spat and scratched wildly at his hands. But the man got his own back. He smiled when he felt the cat's neck break in his huge hands—served him right! He walked quietly to the front door, threw the floppy cat down on the step and took his leave, wiping his hands on his trousers. Blasted rain!

Mrs Morris looked up. She thought she'd heard something. That nice Mr Wilkins had advised her to keep her doors locked, especially at night-time. She got up slowly out of her chair. Her knees felt a bit stiff tonight, and she hobbled to the window and peeped out of the curtains.

It was a nasty night. She saw nothing in the front. It must have been the wind. She peeped through the back kitchen window to see if Kip was sitting on the dustbin. He could be a stupid cat sometimes, but she was a bit worried, knowing he didn't like windy weather. He hadn't come in for his supper, which was unusual too. Maybe he was sheltering somewhere. The wind was getting stronger now. She went back into the front room and pulled her chair up to the fire. *The cat would come home when he was ready,* she thought and carried on watching the news on her tiny television set.

***

Wilkins had received a message as soon as he'd arrived at the station the following morning. Poor Mrs Morris! He knew she'd loved that cat. He hoped Stagg would allow him to visit her straightaway, so he headed to his office.

"Enter!" Stagg said, already seated at his desk. "Ah, Wilkins. Just the chap....'

"Sir, I wonder if I could visit Mrs Morris, sir."

"Not more apple pie, Wilkins?" Stagg smiled.

"No, sir. It's her cat. Someone's left it dead on her front step this morning."

"What? How shocking for her! Yes, certainly you must go. I think I'll come with you, if you don't mind?"

"Yes, sir."

When they arrived at the bungalow, Stagg knocked on the door gently. Mrs Morris answered the door, and Stagg noted her red eyes and the handkerchief half-stuffed up her sleeve.

"Come in," she said.

"I'm sorry to hear about your cat, Mrs Morris. I don't suppose you heard or saw anything?" Stagg sat down on an armchair and smiled kindly. Wilkins sat on the sofa while Mrs Morris sank into her chair. She pulled her handkerchief out of her sleeve.

"No, son, I didn't see anything. I thought I heard something once, but it was so windy last night, I thought it was that. Poor Kip!"

"Yes, it must be very upsetting for you."

"Are you all right, Mrs Morris? Can I get you anything? Or help in any way?" offered Wilkins.

"Well, I suppose you could help me." She looked at the earnest face of the young officer. "I'd like to bury him in the garden, you see. Under the tree. He used to like to watch the birds from there. Watch them all day he would, you know." She chuckled. "He used to take a swipe at them sometimes, but he never caught any. He was too fat; bless him."

Wilkins reached forward and touched her arm. "Of course, Mrs Morris. Where is the old fellow?" He stood up and followed her into the kitchen.

The cat had been carefully wrapped in a small tartan blanket, but the end of his bushy tail peeped through one of the folds.

"Here he is, in his favourite blanket." Mrs Morris pointed to a small tree in the garden. "I thought just under there, love, if that's all right. There's a shovel in the coal kit you can use." She grabbed at his arm as he went out. "You will be careful with him, won't you? I know he's gone, but…." Her voice broke, and Wilkins watched a tear roll down her cheek.

"I will," he said. Wilkins reached down and gently took the tartan bundle into the garden before placing it on the grass. "Just here, Mrs Morris?"

"Yes, just there. And thank you." She turned quickly away and went back inside.

She put the kettle on and called through to Stagg, asking if he'd like a cup of tea. Stagg was sitting upright in an armchair, his hands grasped in front of him, but he stood up and went into the kitchen.

"Yes, if it's not too much trouble. Thank you." He watched her make the tea. "And you said you didn't see anything last night, Mrs Morris?"

"Well, as I said earlier, I thought I heard something, but when I peeped out, I couldn't see anything. It was a terrible night, wasn't it? When I found him this morning, I thought I'd better give you a ring. I just hope he didn't suffer, poor Kip!"

"Yes, you did the right thing. I'll tell an officer to keep a lookout when he does his rounds."

"No, there's no need for that. I'll keep the doors locked, and I know John…erm… I mean Wilkins will pop in to keep a check. Don't you worry about me."

"Yes, but Mrs Morris…." Mrs Morris handed a cup and saucer to Stagg and poured another for Wilkins.

"I have my own suspicions, the same as you, I expect. How cruel to take it out on my cat. Cowards, they are, cowards!" She opened the door. "All done, are you, John? Cup of tea here for you."

CHAPTER 12

The following day was the court case for the jewellery theft. Wilkins had picked up Mrs Morris in plenty of time, and Mr Williams, Miss Ellis and Betty had been picked up by a patrol car. Inspector Stagg and Wilkins took their places near the front of the court, with the witnesses in the row at the back. Bobby and Charley Brooks were sitting in the row opposite, and there were members of the public, along with the local press, in the gallery above. The courtroom was an imposing one, dating from Victorian times. The judge's desk and jury seats were enclosed in carved wooden panelling.

A door opened at the back of the judge's desk, and a clerk called out, "All rise!" Everyone stood up while a robed man entered, nodded to the court and sat down. The others followed suit.

The judge said, "Good morning. Good morning, gentlemen." He addressed the solicitors that were sitting at the front of the court. "We are assembled to hear the case regarding the robbery of jewellery at Williams Jewellers. It is alleged that two men, a Mr Charles Brooks and Mr Robert Brooks entered the shop, threatened and attacked Mr Williams before leaving the premises with several items of jewellery, which as yet, is unrecovered. The police have conducted an identification parade, and I understand that there has been confirmation that the two people who conducted the robbery were Mr Charles Brooks and Mr Robert Brooks, as present in the court here today."

One of the solicitors rose and said, "The confirmation of identification is to be disputed, my lord."

"Indeed," said the judge. "Well, let us proceed. Gentlemen?"

The police solicitor presented their case to the judge and called on their witnesses. Mr Williams relayed what happened on the day of the robbery, adding that his jewellery was still missing. He stared at the Brooks brothers as he left the stand, and they returned his stare without emotion. He nodded to Stagg as he took his seat.

Miss Ellis was next. Her account was almost identical to her employer's, but unlike Mr Williams, she kept her head down and dabbed her nose as she passed the Brooks brothers. She rushed back to her seat, visibly upset.

Betty gave her account of the robbery. Stagg noted that she stated the facts almost in parrot-fashion. He was sure she gave a slight smirk and defiantly lifted her chin as she passed the brothers.

It was Mrs Morris's turn. She kept her account surprisingly to the point but asserted that the men he had seen were the two that were sitting in the dock opposite. As she passed, she glared at them, and Stagg noticed the bigger brother giving her a grin before being nudged in the ribs by his smaller sibling. Mrs Morris marched back to her seat and sat down with a "Humph!"

The police prosecutor concluded that the witness statements, along with the positive identification, proved their case against Charles and Robert Brooks. The police solicitor sat down, and the defence stood up.

"I would like to thank the prosecution for their eloquent presentation of the facts. However, I would like to call Miss Ellis back to the stand, if I may? Thank you." Miss Ellis tottered back to the stand, gripping her handbag tightly. "Now, Miss Ellis, can I confirm a few facts? You said you were in the shop window when it is alleged that my client entered. Is that correct?"

"Yes, sir." Miss Ellis dabbed her nose with her handkerchief.

"Did you have a good view of the assailant?"

"Yes, sir."

"Could you describe him to me, please?"

"Yes. He was a big chap. Tall and stocky, and he had fair hair." Her hands gripped the wooden edge of the stand.

"Did you see his face?"

"Yes. Well, I saw the face with a stocking over it, and he wore a cap." She smiled, trying her best to be helpful.

"So, you didn't actually see his face at all?"

"Yes, I did, but it had a stocking over it."

"Now, Miss Ellis, I want you to take a good look at my client. Are you one hundred per cent sure that this is the man who entered the shop?"

The prosecution solicitor jumped up. "Objection, my lord! Miss Ellis is not to be intimidated by the presence of the alleged assailants. She has already made her identifications at the police station!"

The judge nodded. "This has already been covered by the police report. What is your point?"

"My point, my lord, to beg your pardon, is to ascertain whether the witness is fully confident that her identification is correct."

The judge turned to Miss Ellis. Her eyes were now opened wide, and she was turning her handkerchief over and over in her hands. "Are you all right to proceed, Miss Ellis? I know it must be upsetting for you."

"Yes, sir," Miss Ellis squeaked.

"Very well. Now, if you look at the gentlemen in question, are you certain that these are the men who entered the shop that day? Take your time." Miss Ellis drew her handkerchief to her face and trembled as she peeped over the top at the men in the dock.

The defence solicitor said, "Now, Miss Ellis. Can you say for certain that these are the men?" Miss Ellis squinted across the room, and then she looked down.

"No, I can't," she whispered. Stagg sat upright in his chair and clasped his hands together. He ignored Wilkins' quizzical look.

The defence counsel said, "Thank you, Miss Ellis. You can take a seat. I'd like to call Mr Williams, if I may."

Stagg watched as the defence solicitor went through an almost identical line of questioning with Mr Williams and Betty, drawing the same conclusions. The police prosecution was ineffective. Mrs Morris was next.

The prosecution started. "Now, Mrs Morris, could I ask how old you are?"

"No, you cannot! Most impolite young man!"

She glared at the judge, who said, "Quite right! I do apologise, madam, on behalf of the court. What is your point?" He, too, glared at the defence solicitor.

"I also apologise, Mrs Morris. I didn't mean to cause offence." The defence solicitor glanced down at his papers, much to Mrs Morris's annoyance. "When did you last have your eyes tested, Mrs Morris? Can you remember?" His false smile at the elderly lady in the dock faltered a little when she returned it with a very hard look.

"Of course, I can remember! It was three months ago." She turned to the judge and added, "I go every six months, you see, for a check-up, because of my sugar."

"Your sugar?"

"Yes, I'm a bit diabetic."

"And was your eyesight normal?" asked the defence.

"No, I have to wear glasses."

"Were you wearing your glasses on the day of the robbery?"

"No."

"Were you wearing your spectacles at the identification parade?"

"No, I was not."

"Then I would suggest to the court that if Mrs Morris were not wearing her glasses, it would not have been possible for her to clearly see two men that were over one hundred yards away from her on the day of the robbery. Isn't that right, Mrs Morris?" he added, smiling sweetly.

"No, it isn't! And I would say that you want to check your facts, young man, before you suggest anything!" Mrs Morris snapped. Stifled laughter erupted in the courtroom.

"Order!" the clerk shouted out.

The judge leaned forward. "You are only supposed to respond to questions that are put to you, Mrs Morris!"

"Well, I would if he asked me the right ones!" Loud laughter swept through the court.

"Order!" the clerk shouted again.

"What do you mean exactly, Mrs Morris?" asked the judge.

"I wasn't wearing my glasses on the street because I only need them for reading. I'm long-sighted, you see." She nodded to the courtroom.

"Any more questions?" snapped the judge. The defence persisted with his line of questioning.

"Are you absolutely certain that these were the two men you saw? Absolutely certain?" Mrs Morris glared at the two men. The big one wore a hint of a grin on his face, while the other just stared ahead with watery eyes. She hesitated. "Well? The court is waiting, Mrs Morris," the defence said.

"If I saw them again on the street, I would be a hundred per cent sure. But in this courtroom, in their suits, they look different. I'm almost certain it's them."

"And the registration number? Did you see that clearly?"

"Yes, I've told you."

"Thank you, Mrs Morris. You may leave the dock."

Mrs Morris marched past the two men and took her seat. She mouthed, "Sorry!" to Wilkins as she sat down.

The solicitor summed up his case for the defence, and the court was adjourned until after lunch. Stagg and Wilkins waited in an office outside the courtroom with their witnesses while the Brooks brothers went across the road to a pub. Stagg hoped that their lunchtime drinks would be their last for some time.

Everyone was called back into the court, and they rose when the judge entered and then sat down once again.

"I have carefully considered this case. I have considered the witness statements, the results of the identification parade, and the cases put forward by the prosecution and the defence. It is my judgement that there is insufficient evidence to conclusively convict Mr Charles Brooks and Mr Robert Brooks for the jewellery robbery in question, and as such, they are free to leave the court. Good afternoon."

Miss Ellis and Wilkins both gasped at the same time.

Mrs Morris shouted, "The blighters have got away with it!"

"Order!" the clerk shouted as the judge left the court, but his demands were muffled by the whoops of joy from the gallery as the two brothers left the court.

Stagg stood up, and Mrs Morris said, "I'm sorry, son. I did see them, but they looked different in court in their suits, and that solicitor twisted my words."

"That's all right, Mrs Morris. Not to worry. Are you all right? Wilkins will take you home, won't you?"

"Yes, I will. Come on, Mrs Morris, maybe we'll have a nice cup of tea. I could do with one, couldn't you?"

Wilkins chatted to Mrs Morris as he left the courtroom but nodded at Stagg as he passed. Stagg followed them outside.

The two brothers were on the steps of the court, and they were giving their account of the case to the local press. There were smiles from their friends that were gathered around them, with mention of *"having a good drink tonight to celebrate."* They glared at Stagg as he passed them, and he heard them mention *"Victimisation!"* to the keen reporters who were busy snapping with their cameras.

As Stagg expected, the chief had gone mad over the case, accusing Stagg of producing insufficient evidence. Burns had added fuel to the fire accusing Stagg of giving false assurances that the two felons would be convicted. It was an open-and-shut case. Only it wasn't, was it?

Burns added that unless Stagg's performance improved, he would seriously have to re-evaluate his current position as an inspector. Stagg knew that he couldn't be demoted unless there was a serious breach of conduct, and that wasn't going to happen. Stagg was annoyed himself over the court's verdict but knew he couldn't alter it.

Things didn't get any better when the court case was featured in the local paper a couple of days later.

"Stagg! Have you seen it in all the papers? Makes us look like bloody idiots! And those Brooks brothers, smirking about it. You keep a sharp eye on those two. They're not making fools of us, Stagg. A sharp eye, mind. Anything at all, I don't care!"

"Sir!" Stagg managed to utter before the chief rang off. Hudson appeared at the door.

"Cup of tea, sir?"

"I need more than tea, Hudson!" Stagg glared at the phone before replacing the receiver.

"Everything all right?" Hudson asked.

"Yes, not to worry. It'll blow over, I expect," Stagg sighed.

"Is it to do with the Brooks court case, sir?"

"Sort of. Any of those ginger nuts left?'" He smiled at her, pushing back his hair.

"I'll find some for you." Stagg sat back in his chair and sighed.

The next day was taken up with car thefts, some drunken arrests after a football match, and a report of a peeping-tom: just routine work. Even though the court case had allegedly proved otherwise, Stagg was still sure the Brooks brothers were guilty of the jewellery robbery and possibly others in the area. There was also Kip, the cat. Was that just a coincidence, or was Mrs Morris right? Were the Brooks brothers behind it?

Stagg had another chat with Hudson to see if she was prepared to do some more observation work on Betty. She agreed.

On Saturday, Stagg picked Hudson up, went to The White Lion, and followed the same procedure as before. This time they were lucky. It was another rainy night. Betty shook her fair hair as she entered, screwing up her nose. Hudson thought she looked a lot younger than when she was in the shop. Another woman was with her who was of similar build. Maybe it was her sister. They were laughing as they went to the bar, and it was obvious they had had a few drinks already. They carried their glasses past Hudson and sat down on the other side of the room.

Hudson went to the bar to see if she could get a better view. Betty and her friend were sitting at a small table in the corner. They fell about in fits of laughter at a private joke and downed their drinks. Hudson was about to order when a voice said in her ear, "Here again, are you? I haven't seen you for a while. What will you have, darling?" A thin man motioned to the barman.

"Two brandies, a pint, and whatever the lady's having."

Hudson, surprised, didn't reply immediately. The barman busied himself while the thin man said, "Have you made your mind up, or do you always play hard to get?"

"I'll have a gin and tonic," snapped Hudson. She might learn a bit more about Betty for Stagg.

"That's my girl! Glad you know what's good for you!" The man placed a finger on the side of his nose. "Mum's the word. The wife's over there. Maybe we could meet up again sometime. I like a girl with class, not that there's much in here."

"Thanks for the drink," Hudson said, returning to her seat. The thin man watched her look at her watch. It was almost ten o'clock.

Hudson slowly drank her gin and tonic. The thin man went to the bar again about ten minutes later. Hudson avoided his gaze and looked at her watch again, hoping to give the impression that she was waiting for someone. She decided to pop to the loo before calling it a night, but as she was making her way back to the lounge, the thin man blocked her path.

"Not going yet, are you? I thought we were going to get to know each other a bit better." He slipped his arm around her waist.

"No. I don't think that's a good idea," Hudson said, stepping back.

"No? Too good for me, are you?" His lip curled with anger.

"No!" Hudson whispered. "You said your wife was here."

The man stepped back a little, then smiled. "I knew you were my sort as soon as I set eyes on you. I said, didn't I, Reg?" The landlord nodded, and the thin man smiled at Hudson while looking her up and down. He leaned forward. "You're right about my missus. She gets a bit jealous, you know. Here's my card. Give me a ring tomorrow, darling. I don't want to keep you waiting." Hudson smiled at him but strolled back to her seat.

She finished her drink, grabbed her coat, and left, walking around the corner and up the road. She walked on for about five minutes and then waited. It was still raining when Stagg picked her up.

"All good?"

"Yes, sir. All good. Chips tonight again, sir?"

"Yes, Hudson. Chips it is." He drove a while before asking, "Well? I saw Betty go in. Who did she speak to?"

"She was with another woman. A relative, I would say, as she looked quite similar. They were both a bit drunk. It was funny, really, because they were sitting with that chap who tried it on with me last time. It turns out he's Betty's friend's husband."

"Is he now? Did you go to the bar?"

"Yes, I did, sir. He offered to buy me a drink, and I accepted." Hudson turned her face to the window. The thought of the man disgusted her. Stagg glanced at her.

"Did you? Why?"

"Well, I thought I might be able to find out a bit more information."

"And did you?"

"Not really. Only that he's married, and he wants to meet me again. He gave me his card with his number and wants me to phone him tomorrow, sir."

"Ah! So that's why you flew out of the pub. You looked as if the devil himself was after you, Hudson." She laughed a little but then fell silent while Stagg continued to drive.

"Look, Hudson, I don't want you to come here again. It was only a hunch I had, that's all. Nothing definite to go on, really."

"No, you're wrong, sir. I think you are on the right track. I don't mind helping you. It's just that chap, sir. He gives me the creeps."

"Well, that's okay, Hudson. Thank you. But you're not going there again," Stagg declared. "Now, what do you want with your chips?"

"I'll leave them, if you don't mind, sir."

"Oh, are you sure? I haven't offended you, have I?"

"No, I'm fine, really. Just not very hungry."

Stagg dropped her off home, and she ran inside. Stagg was angry at himself. He shouldn't have asked her to go out on a stakeout for him. He was surprised at his anger at the thought of someone making a pass at her. It was a long time since he and Hazel had split up. He should have asked her out properly, maybe to go to a restaurant, not fish and chips. She was a nice girl. He decided to ask her soon. He did enjoy Hudson's company.

CHAPTER 13

The next day, Hudson decided to phone the man she'd met in the pub. She'd been thinking about it all night and was confident she could handle the man's advances. Inspector Stagg had been disappointed that the court case had been thrown out on a technicality, but Hudson was determined to help. She hadn't been in court herself, but she'd seen the tightness of Inspector Stagg's lips when he'd returned. He was busy today, tidying up some reports with Wilkins, so Hudson didn't have a chance to give him the man's business card.

At four o'clock, Hudson noticed Stagg leaving his office. She wanted to give him the man's business card, but as she stood up, her phone rang. By the time she'd finished the call, he had gone.

Stagg was on his way to visit the Baines factory again, and he arrived in the yard just as some of the workers started to leave. A couple of men were talking by a car, and Stagg noticed the car had a puncture.

"Do you need a hand?" Stagg asked. "That's as flat as a pancake!"

"I know. Blasted thing!" said one of the men.

The other man said, "It's okay. We should manage it." He pulled a wrench out of the car boot and squatted down by the wheel.

"All right, as long as you're sure? It's just what you need before you go home, isn't it?"

The man pulled off the tyre, and the other man passed him the spare one.

"You all right, now, Graham? Only I've got to get home handy tonight. The missus is going out."

"Yes, thanks, Tom." Graham pushed the tyre into place. "There! That should do it. It's my second puncture in the last two weeks, you know!"

"Oh, that is bad luck," said Stagg.

"Are you here for a job or something?"

"No, no. I just wanted a word with Mr Baines."

"Oh, well, I think you've missed him. I saw his Jag leaving about ten minutes ago."

"Oh, that's a nuisance. I wanted to know whether he knew a chap I was looking for. An old acquaintance—Charley Brooks."

"Charley Brooks? That waste of space? He was in school with me. A bit older than me, he was. A right rogue and all."

"Have you ever seen him here?"

"Oh yes, he used to come here regular. Once a month, I think. Odd jobs, Mr Baines said. Odd jobs. Huh!"

"So, you don't think he was doing actual work then?"

The man stood up. "I don't know. Who are you anyway asking all these questions?"

"I'm Inspector Stagg. Sorry, I should have mentioned that earlier."

"Oh, police, eh? Well, no harm done. No. I don't know what he used to do for Mr Baines, but whatever it was, it didn't take him long. He was always in and out in about ten minutes flat. Well, I must be going. Goodnight, sir."

"Goodnight."

Stagg headed for home. His head was full of information, and he felt weary. He must get that man's business card from Hudson tomorrow.

***

At Hudson's home, Pamela had been thinking about how she would get some more information for Adam Stagg. Not that she'd ever called Inspector Stagg by his first name. It had been lovely lately, going out on stakeouts with him. Even though they had talked briefly, she had felt closer to him. She was sure he was a bit friendlier towards her, or was it her imagination? And if she could help him with this case, who knows what might happen between them then? Maybe they would start going out properly. She smiled.

Hudson dialled the number on The Iron Jim business card and recognised the voice when he answered. She shuddered.

"Hello. It's me. You gave me your number last night."

"I knew you wouldn't be able to resist," the man sneered. "Where do you fancy going, darling? We can't go to The White

Lion. Do you know the Royal Oak on Wenbury Road? It's a couple of miles out of town, but it's nice. I'll meet you there tonight at eight."

"Tonight?"

"Yes. I know you can't wait to see me, darling."

"Well, I….'

"Well?"

"Yes, all right then. Eight it is." Hudson felt sick. Maybe she should tell Stagg after all, but he'd probably talk her out of it, so she decided against it and ran upstairs to get ready.

***

At eight o'clock, the taxi dropped her off at the Royal Oak. It had been a lovely pub in its heyday but now looked in desperate need of a coat of paint. She stepped inside, and the smell of stale cigarettes and old beer filled her nostrils. It was a dark shabby bar with black stools and copper-topped tables crammed into a tiny room. A couple of chaps nursed their pints by the bar and looked her up and down.

In her ear, a voice whispered, "So you're here at last." She turned to see the thin man dressed in trousers and a cotton shirt. *'No tracksuit tonight,'* Hudson thought as he put his arm around her waist.

"Come on, let's sit down. What is it, darling? Brandy or whiskey?"

"I'll have a Babycham, please," said Hudson, clutching her bag. She escaped his grip and took a seat near the window.

"No, come over here, near the fire. It's cosier, if you know what I mean."

Hudson didn't want to be cosy with this man, but she sat in a chair near the fire. He put her drink on the table and sat next to her.

"Cheers!" he said, clinking her glass. "You're looking lovely tonight, by the way!" She felt his breath on her cheek as he whispered in her ear. "Nice change from the missus, if you know what I mean." Hudson sipped her drink. "Go on, get it down you. Plenty of time for more. Come on! I'll get us another."

Hudson gulped down her drink and smiled. She thought she could be voted the best actress of the year. She needed to keep her wits about her and try to find out as much information as she could. The man returned with more drinks and placed her glass on the table. Sitting next to her, he gently stroked her thigh. She cringed inwardly and sipped the pale liquid.

"Like the boots, by the way," he whispered in her ear. "I'm looking forward to taking them off later, darling."

Hudson took another drink. "Now, now, cheeky!" she said, moving his hand. "We don't want anyone seeing us, do we?"

"No, you're right! Maybe we should go somewhere quieter."

"No, not yet," Hudson said. She hadn't thought that he might suggest going elsewhere. Maybe she should have told Stagg about this meeting. "I'm just getting warm." She reached her hands out to the open fire.

"Better get you a brandy then to go with the Babycham." He trotted back to the bar.

Hudson glanced around the room. Two old men played dominoes at a corner table, and a couple sat near the window, engrossed in each other. Hudson thought she should phone Stagg as soon as she could. The man returned with a brandy, and Hudson knew it was going to be a bit tricky shaking him off.

"There you go. Don't want you to get cold now, do we?" He was so smug.

"Have you been busy today?"

"What do you mean?"

"Just wondered, that's all. You're a businessman, aren't you?" Hudson sipped her drink.

"Yes, I am, but I don't mix business with pleasure." He gripped her thigh, and Hudson felt sick. She stood up.

"Just need to powder my nose."

She stepped past him and was glad of the coolness of the ladies toilet. She would go back and say she didn't feel very well, then go home. She sighed. She hadn't found out anything new to tell Stagg. She looked at her flushed face, noting she must have been too near the fire, after all.

CHAPTER 14

The next morning, a WPC appeared at Stagg's office door. He'd asked for an update on some checks.

"That was quick, Hudson," he said, then blushed when he saw it was WPC Jones. "Ah, Jones! Sorry about that. I thought….'

"Yes, sir. Hudson's phoned in sick. I'm doing the checks today, sir."

"Hudson's sick? Not serious, I hope?"

"She didn't say, sir. She sounded very quiet, though."

"I see."

***

The next morning, Stagg looked up as WPC Jones came into his office with a cup of tea.

"Thank you. Is Hudson still not in, Jones?" Stagg sipped his tea, avoiding her gaze.

"No, sir. It's funny for her to be off. It must be a nasty tummy bug. I might phone her tonight to see how she is, sir."

"Indeed. Yes. Good idea."

Jones rolled her eyes as she left his office. She didn't know Stagg was sorry that his best roses had finished flowering, or he could have picked some for Hudson.

***

The next day, Stagg and Wilkins were barely through the station's door when WPC Jones dashed up to them. Stagg could see she was upset.

"It's Hudson, sir. I think she's gone missing!" she blurted out.

"What do you mean? You'd better come into my office, Jones." Stagg closed the door. "Right! Now, what's all this about Hudson going missing."

"Well, sir, I phoned Pam's house last night. Her mum was surprised when I asked for her. She said she'd had a phone call from here to say she'd been put on special training and wouldn't be home for a few days. Her mum thought it was a bit funny because she hadn't taken any clothes with her. But she isn't on special training, sir, is she?"

"No, Jones, she isn't."

"No, that's what I thought. I know she had a boyfriend who lived away. Perhaps she's gone to see him, sir. But she'd told me it was over with him ages ago. Maybe I'm panicking, sir."

"A boyfriend, eh?" Stagg grunted. "Well, Jones, maybe it's just that. Not to worry."

"But it's just not like her to take time off and say nothing to me, sir. That's why I am worried!"

"Okay, Jones, don't panic. Now, did Hudson mention anything out of the ordinary to you lately?"

"No, sir. I can't remember anything in particular. Only the case you'd been working on, the jewellery robbery case, but I can't exactly remember what she said, sir." The WPC sank into the chair.

"I see." Stagg gripped his finger under his chin.

"Pam told me she'd been to The White Lion for a couple of drinks, and she'd seen someone there that had given her the creeps."

"Well, can you think of anything else, Jones?" Stagg leant forward, hopeful.

"I'm sorry. I can't remember anything else, sir."

"Okay, Jones. Let me know if she phones, won't you? She may be with her ex-boyfriend, as you said."

"Sir." The WPC left the office, and Stagg could see she was worried.

Stagg wracked his brains. Where had Hudson gone? Should he start a search? Was she taking an unplanned holiday for a few days? She'd said she didn't have a boyfriend, but the thought of that upset Stagg more than he was prepared to acknowledge. He'd have to visit Hudson's mother. She'd know her daughter's whereabouts, surely?

***

Hudson opened her eyes. Her head was pounding as she struggled to focus on her surroundings. She tried to lift herself up but felt herself falling. Blackness overcame her as she slipped in and out of consciousness. Hudson's head had turned into a huge roaring engine. She slowly opened her eyes again, afraid of making the noise worse. She kept her head still and looked up. A ceiling stained yellow with old nicotine loomed above her. She turned her head slightly and strained to hear if anyone else was in the room, but her ears seemed to be blocked.

Hudson rolled quietly onto her side with her eyes closed and waited a few seconds in case someone was watching her. No one came, and no one shouted at her. Her head was still pounding. She opened her eyes and turned over on her other side.

The room only had one window, set up high in the wall. She must be in a basement. She looked across the room to the door. Carefully she prised herself up off the bed. She waited. Her head felt as if it was going to fall off, and when she tried to stand up, her legs were wobbly. She sat back on the bed for a few moments.

"Steady now. Come on, Hudson!" she said aloud.

Finding her balance, she stepped slowly towards the door. The floor was freezing under her feet, and God knows where her boots were. She pulled on the door handle but knew it would be locked. Sweat trickled down the back of her neck, and the rushing noise in her ears became unbearable. She staggered back to the bed and gripped the grimy blankets before finally passing out.

***

The next day, Jones told Stagg that she'd managed to contact Hudson's ex-boyfriend. He hadn't seen her for months. Stagg left the station, closely followed by Wilkins.

"Where are we going, sir? To tell the chief?"

"We'd better go to see Hudson's mother first. She's probably worried sick."

"Yes, yes, sir. Of course, she must be. She's a nice girl, Hudson."

"Yes, she's a nice lady." Stagg gripped the steering wheel and, picking up speed, stared grimly ahead.

As they travelled, Wilkins thought about the gossip amongst the WPCs—about Stagg and Hudson. Some had said it was unrequited love on Hudson's part, with Stagg being as exciting as a block of wood. Wilkins noted Stagg's furrowed brow and decided that maybe Stagg wasn't as wooden as they'd all thought.

The car turned into a cul-de-sac of neat semis, and they soon knocked on the door. A small woman with greying hair that had once been dark appeared. Wilkins could see the family resemblance.

"Any news?" she said as Stagg strode up the path.

"No, I'm afraid not. May we come in, Mrs Hudson?" Stagg said gently. He could see her eyes were red.

"Yes, of course. Inspector Stagg, isn't it? Pamela has mentioned you."

"Yes, I'm Stagg, and this is Wilkins." Stagg was trying his best to keep things formal, but inside he felt frantic. "Now, tell me what Hudson, eh, Pamela, said the last time you saw her."

"Well, she just said she was going out again. I thought she was going with you. You know, like the other week. She'd been so pleased that you'd asked her to help you." Wilkins glanced at Stagg, who said nothing. "I saw you drop her off, you see, so she explained," Mrs Hudson added. Wilkins' eyebrows arched.

"Did she say where she was going?" Stagg asked.

"No. But she was dressed up. That's why I thought she was going out with you."

"What was she wearing?" Stagg knew he sounded unsympathetic, but he couldn't help himself.

Mrs Hudson got her handkerchief out and blew her nose before giving him a brief description of Pamela's outfit. She knew from her daughter that Inspector Stagg was a stickler for detail.

"It was only when Diane phoned for Pamela that I realised something was wrong. Where do you think she's gone?"

"I'm not sure, Mrs Hudson. Don't worry. We'll have her home before you know it." He got up, closely followed by Wilkins.

"I hope so. I'm so worried! I was hoping you'd sent her on a special mission," she half-joked as he stepped outside.

"Special mission?" asked Stagg, turning around.

"Yes, she said you'd asked her to do some special work for you or something."

"Yes, that's right, yes. I'll be in touch, Mrs Hudson, as soon as I find her." They got back in the car, and Stagg was conscious of his fellow officer's gaze. "Don't even ask, Wilkins!"

***

If they'd only known the 'special' mission Hudson had undertaken, they'd have been mortified. It wasn't going as planned. Pamela Hudson opened her eye and immediately knew that someone was in the room with her as she could hear them at the foot of the bed. She carefully turned her head to see the thin man grinning at her.

"So, you've woken up at last, darling."

Hudson tried to speak, but her mouth was dry. She croaked, "Where am I? What's going on?" She tried to prop herself up, and the thin man quickly put his arm under her shoulders to help her.

"There. That's it. You sit up a bit."

She tried to push him away. "Get off me!" Her shout was no more than a whisper.

"Oh, charming, that is, I must say! And there's me thinking you'd want a drink and all." He moved away.

Hudson could see that he had a carrier bag with him. Her throat felt on fire, and she needed a drink. She decided she'd try her best to reason with him but still felt very weak.

"Could I have a drink, please?"

"That's better. I knew you were my sort of girl." She watched him pour out some water for her and grabbed at the glass, drinking the contents. "Steady!" the man said, sitting on the bed. He took the glass from her.

Hudson knew she might have a chance of escaping if she played along. But she found it difficult not to hit him when he placed his hand on her thigh, smiling at her with yellow teeth.

"What about a kiss?" He leant forward.

Hudson moved away. "A kiss? After the way you're treating me? I thought you were a successful businessman—Charles Brooks, with a fancy business card. I thought you were different. But you're not, are you? You're like all the rest of them!" She turned away from him, hoping he'd be taken in. The thin man narrowed his eyes, stared at her, then got up.

"How do you know I'm Charley Brooks? It doesn't say on the card."

"The landlord in the pub told me."

"Reg? I don't believe you. But you're right. I'm not like the rest of them. You'll see, darling, you'll see." He picked up the glass and placed it in a carrier bag. Hudson's vision blurred as she heard him saying, "Sweet dreams, darling. Sweet dreams."

CHAPTER 15

That night, Stagg went to The White Lion but didn't see anyone of interest. The chief had wanted to make a statement to the papers about Hudson, but Stagg had persuaded him not to. Hudson's safety could be put in peril. Stagg was working flat out to see if there were any leads, and all the staff at the station were put on alert. He decided to stay at the station in case any news came in.

Unbeknown to Stagg, Wilkins had decided to conduct his own investigations. He visited a couple of pubs in Whytfield, always on the lookout for anything suspicious. He thought he caught sight of Stagg at The Oak, but if he had, he didn't catch up with him.

At The White Lion, Wilkins gave up drinking ginger beer and had a couple of pints. He thought he saw Betty with some other people, but by the time he'd been served by the landlord, they'd left. He noticed there were a couple of the gipsies in one corner as he stood by the bar, as well as several local chaps.

It was a shame he hadn't been able to come up with anything to help the investigation. He enjoyed working with Inspector Stagg and was glad his uncle had put him with him and not Burns.

He didn't care much for his attitude and thought he was big-headed. Stagg was a completely different kettle of fish. He treated everyone with respect and hadn't teased Wilkins about being the chief's nephew. Wilkins knew him well enough now to know he was worried sick about Hudson.

He did wonder what the 'special work' was, though. Was it Stagg's way of getting to know Hudson better, or the other way around? He had noticed her watching Stagg a couple of times like girls do sometimes.

Wilkins thought about his ex-girlfriend, Hannah. They'd met when he was still training a few months back. She was going to become a teacher. They'd argued and parted because Hannah had said he wasn't serious enough about her. Perhaps he hadn't been.

Wilkins drank his beer, thinking how he would feel if Hannah went missing. His stomach churned at the thought of it. He didn't think she was going out with anyone else, and he did miss her a lot more than he'd thought he would. Maybe he'd give her a ring tomorrow.

At ten-thirty, he left the pub and started to walk home. He didn't live too far out of town, so he'd decided not to take the car. He turned briskly down Bear Alley, one of the several alleys that led off the high street, to cut through to Severn Street. He hadn't been sure of what he might discover, but as Stagg said, any information is important. He started to whistle as he went along, and then everything went black.

***

When he came around, all Wilkins could hear was shouting.

"It's that copper. The police. Quick! Phone for an ambulance." Wilkins opened his eyes and saw the gipsy man who owned the green car.

He stuttered, "I'm sorry, I…." Then he passed out.

Wilkins came around properly the following day. He was in hospital, and his mother was sitting at his bedside.

"Oh, John, you're awake. How do you feel? Does your head hurt?" Wilkins struggled to sit up, and his mother immediately started tugging at his pillows.

"I'm all right, Mother. Don't fuss!"

"I'm not fussing. And if this is what police work gets you, you can get another job!"

"Now, Mother, please."

Someone coughed politely and said, "How are you, Wilkins?"

"Inspector, sir! Mother, this is Inspector Stagg."

"Yes, I know who he is. Now, is there anything you need, son?"

"No, I don't. I'm hoping to come out today. I'll see you later, Mother. You can go now."

"But John...."

"Don't worry. I'll be fine." Mrs Wilkins shook her head and took her leave.

Stagg sat down. "What happened?"

"I was cutting through Bear Alley, just off the high street, sir. When I got through the other side, someone hit me over the head. I came to a bit and saw that gipsy chap."

"Yes, one of the constables detained him."

"Oh, I see."

"Why? Is there a problem, Wilkins?"

"I don't know. I need to sort this out." Wilkins sat up straight and swung his legs out of bed. His head still ached a bit, and he felt a bit dizzy.

Stagg grabbed his arm. "You stay here a while longer, Wilkins. There's no rush. I'll sort it out at the station. You have a rest."

Wilkins sat back against his pillows and said weakly, "Okay, yes, I think I will, sir. Just for a while." Wilkins noted the dark circles under Stagg's eyes.

"Any news on Hudson, sir?"

"Not yet. Hopefully, we'll hear something soon. Make sure you rest, Wilkins. I'm off now." Stagg stood up.

"Yes. Bye, sir."

"Bye."

Stagg already knew that Wilkins had a concussion and had doubted the night desk sergeant's decision to detain the gipsy. He had a word with the ward sister and made sure Wilkins wouldn't be allowed out of hospital until the following day.

Stagg strode out of the hospital. When he returned to the station, he asked to see Leo, the gipsy, in the police cells.

Leo was sitting upright on the wooden bench in the police cell. He stood up when Stagg opened the door.

"At last! Are you going to let me out? I've got things to do, you know."

"Yes, sir. Just tell me what happened last night." Stagg sat down on the bench.

"I've already told you lot. We came out the pub, me and Sam, and cut through the alley to get home. Your mate was lying face down, moaning."

"Did you see or hear anything else?"

"I didn't, but I think Sam said he saw someone running off down Severn Street. I sent Sam back into the pub to get an ambulance. When the police turned up, Sam ran off, and I was arrested and slammed in here. Put them straight, will you? I should be working today for food for my family."

"You're sure you didn't have anything to do with this?"

"Yes, I am. That's right, blame us gipsy folk. You're no different to any of the others."

"Bit of a coincidence, isn't it, that you were going the same way as the police officer?"

"I tell you, it wasn't us that hit him!" Leo leaned back in his chair and fiddled with his fingers. He sighed. "All right, we were following him. We were going to frighten him a bit, that's all."

"Oh? And how were you going to do that? Not by beating him up, surely?"

"No! I tell you, we didn't have anything to do with that. No, all we were going to do was make a few creepy noises by the big trees at the graveyard. And that's all! But when we turned down the alley, we saw this chap hitting him, so we shouted and ran to him, and that's the truth."

"And you didn't see the man's face?"

"No, I didn't. But he was a big chap. That's all I can say. Now when am I getting out of here?" Leo paced up and down like a cat in a cage.

"Why didn't you tell us this before?"

"Because your lot didn't give me a chance, and you wouldn't believe me anyway, you never do. He'd have been a lot worse off if I had hit him."

"You should tell the truth, Leo. Lies don't help anyone."

"That's as may be. Why would I wait for the ambulance to arrive if I'd hit him, eh? Don't be stupid."

"All right. You'll have to stay in a bit longer."

"Why?"

"Because I have to sort out some paperwork first. Calm down and be patient a while longer."

Stagg left the cell and returned to the main desk. He asked Sergeant Roberts for the previous night's reports and skimmed through them.

"Sergeant Hughes was on duty last night, was he? Unusual to detain a witness, isn't it?"

"Yes, I thought that myself! Mind you, I don't trust them. He is a gipsy, sir."

"Yes, he is, but that's no reason to automatically detain him for no reason, Roberts, as you well know."

"I believe Inspector Burns instructed the sergeant to detain the lad, sir."

"Inspector Burns? What was he doing here that late? I didn't know he was here."

"Oh, I don't know, sir, and I don't think Hughes wanted to ask him, really. Sergeant Hughes didn't know you were still here, sir, or he'd have checked with you."

"Right! We have no reason to detain him, so release him straightaway, please. I have a witness statement from him and apologise, please, Roberts."

"But, sir! What about Inspector Burns? What will he say?"

"Don't worry, Roberts, I'll take full responsibility."

Stagg entered his office and sat down. Still no news on Hudson, and now Wilkins was beaten up. They must be getting close.

CHAPTER 16

The next morning, Burns poked his head around Stagg's door.

"Well, this is a turn-up for the books, a missing WPC. That nice dark one too. Your assistant was knocked out, and you let the prime suspect go after I detained him. Think you know what you're doing, Stagg? If you need any help, just let me know. I always do a job properly. Huh!" he grunted and left.

Stagg closed his eyes. He knew very well that Burns had always seemed to solve every case he had followed. Stagg's brow furrowed. Just then, Wilkins walked into his office, sporting a large sticking plaster on his head.

"Wilkins! Are you feeling better?"

"Yes, much better, sir, thank you. Did you get that chap released? I wanted to thank him for helping me the other night."

"Yes, I did. I sorted that out yesterday for you. You're sure they weren't involved, Wilkins?"

"Definitely, because they were still in the pub when I left, sir."

"Yes, that's what they said. I'm just going to the gipsy camp now. You can come with me if you like. We need to speak to a lad called Sam."

"Sam?"

"Yes, he was the one who phoned for an ambulance while Leo held you up, I believe."

Wilkins looked down. "I owe them a lot. It's a good job they came along when they did."

Stagg glanced at Wilkins and smiled. "Yes, it was."

They arrived at the camp and were greeted by Ralph. His eyes narrowed a little when he saw Wilkins, but he waved to them both. Leo appeared from behind one of the vans and was taken aback when Wilkins dashed up to him.

"Hello. Look, I just wanted to thank you for helping me last night, Leo. It was very kind of you, especially after what I said about your car being involved in a crime. It was wrong of me, and I'm sorry."

Leo coldly stared at the fair-headed young man who had grabbed his hand, shaking it vigorously. Then his face broke into a smile.

"That's all right. Least we could do. I see you're back to normal now."

"Is Sam about, Ralph?" Stagg asked.

A dark-headed young lad sheepishly peeped out from the back of one of the caravans.

"Here!" he shouted and jumped down the steps. He looked about sixteen.

"What did you see last night in the alley, Sam?"

"We saw the copper going down the alley and thought we'd follow him for a bit. Besides, it was on our way home, wasn't it, Leo?"

"Yes, that's right."

"Anyway, he went down the alley, and we followed a couple of minutes after. It was a good job, 'cos I think the chap would have hit him again."

"Can you describe the person?"

"Not really. It was too dark. He was quite a hefty bloke. Not overly tall but chunky. Wore a donkey jacket and a woolly hat."

"Would you recognise him again?" Stagg asked.

"No, it was too dark, mate," Sam said.

"What did he hit him with?"

"Oh, I think he just hit him. Not with anything, just his fists. Mind you, it wouldn't take much to knock him out, would it?" He nodded to Wilkins and laughed.

"Sam! That'll do," shouted Ralph.

"That's all right. Thank you, anyway," Wilkins said.

"Yes, thanks again and sorry about the misunderstanding." Stagg nodded and walked back to his car.

"Now, if you're up to it, Wilkins, I've decided to revisit the jewellers."

"Lead the way, sir. Any news on Hudson, sir?"

"Not yet. Wilkins, not yet."

Wilkins and Stagg walked in just as Miss Ellis was wiping down a glass-fronted cabinet.

"Oh, Inspector! Hello there," she called out. "Mr Williams, the police are here." The jeweller peeped out from the back room.

"Any news on my jewellery yet, Inspector?" He held a gold watch in his hand. Stagg had almost forgotten about the stolen jewellery.

"No sir, I'm still pursuing my enquiries, I'm afraid."

"I see. Well, how can we help you today, Inspector?"

"I'd like to have a word with Betty if I may. Is she in?"

"Actually, we'd like to have a word with that girl as well!" Miss Ellis huffed.

"Now, now, Miss Ellis," warned Mr Williams.

"Why? Has something happened?" asked Stagg.

"She's finished. Just like that! Didn't even work her notice. Said she had a job to go to and that she had to start there immediately, or she'd lose it. *"Chance of a lifetime,"* she'd said, didn't she, Mr Williams?"

"Yes, that's what she said, Inspector."

"When was this?" asked Wilkins before Stagg had a chance.

"It was this morning, actually. We shall have to advertise in the Labour Exchange now, just when she was settling in too. I don't know what's the matter with these girls nowadays." Miss Ellis twisted her duster as if she was twisting Betty's neck.

"Indeed," said Stagg. "I don't suppose she told you where her new job was going to be, did she?"

"I can't remember. I think it may have been a bank. No. It was a Building Society, I think, yes, I'm almost sure it was. Sorry, I can't remember, Inspector,"

"Don't worry, Miss Ellis. I wonder, though, if you could give me her address. You do have that, I trust?"

"Yes, we do. We've got to send her insurance card to her. I'll just note it down for you," said Mr Williams. He went into the back room and returned a few moments later with the details.

"Thank you. I'll be in touch as soon as I find any more information. Oh, this building society, was it in Whytfield?"

"Yes, it was. She can't drive, you see. Well, goodbye. Thank you, and good luck with finding my stock," said the jeweller.

When he returned to the station, Stagg asked Wilkins to phone the two building societies in Whytfield to see if they'd recently recruited a young woman.

"And I'd give them a description of Betty, if I were you, just in case she's using a different name."

"Yes, sir," said Wilkins. He looked a bit pale.

"You okay, Wilkins? Have a cup of tea and sit down for a bit."

"Yes, sir. Thanks. I'll make those calls at the same time, sir."

"Good. Carry on." As Stagg went back to his office, he caught sight of WPC Jones. "Any news?" he asked.

"No, sir, not yet." Her face looked grim.

"Right. Wilkins? Can you come into my office, please?"

"Sir."

"Wilkins, I want you to start on the missing person's procedure on Hudson straightaway. I'm going to The White Lion again to do some checks myself. You can start things off for me here."

"Yes, if you're sure, yes, sir."

Stagg was just leaving the station when Jones shouted, "Sir. Phone call for you."

Stagg knew who it would be. "Stagg here."

"Any news on WPC Hudson? Put everyone available on the search. We can't have police going missing. What would the papers say? It was bad enough with that court case. I'm very disappointed, Stagg, very disappointed!" The chief didn't pause to draw breath. Stagg said nothing. There was no point.

"Stagg? Are you still there?"

"Yes, sir. I have already asked Wilkins to start the procedure, sir. We....'

"Well, it's a good job you've got help, isn't it, Stagg? Tsk!"

***

At The White Lion, Stagg had Hudson's staff photo in his pocket and showed it to the landlord. He peered at the photo.

"Yes, she does look a bit familiar. She wasn't in her uniform, though, when I saw her."

"When was that?" Stagg said, watching him keenly.

"Oh, I dunno for sure." The landlord scratched his head, squinting at the photo. "We get a lot of youngsters in here, you know. I think it was when we were busy. Yes, it must have been darts night. So that would make it Monday. A policewoman, was she?" He handed the photo back and carefully wiped a glass.

"I don't suppose you remember if she was with anyone?" Stagg asked, ignoring his question.

"No, she was definitely on her own."

"I thought you said you couldn't remember?" Stagg said, leaning forward.

"Well, now I think about it, that's right, it looked as if she was waiting for someone. It got crowded in here afterwards, so I didn't notice her leaving. Sorry."

"You're sure you didn't see anyone with her? It's important."

"No. I didn't. I told you."

"I see," Stagg put the photo back into his pocket. He jotted his number down on a leaf from his notebook and gave it to the landlord. "Here's my number if you remember anything at all."

"Okay, sir."

Stagg went out the door and waited outside for a few moments before tip-toeing back in. He heard the landlord on the phone.

"No, Charlie. I didn't say anything, honest. But you'd better be careful, mate. I'll keep you posted, yes." The landlord rang off and turned to see Stagg standing by the bar. "Oh my god!" His face turned pale.

"Who were you phoning? Tell me, and be quick about it, or you'll be on a charge!" Stagg growled.

"I dunno what you mean," stuttered the landlord.

"Well, you'd better remember, hadn't you, and quick. We can soon check your phone records, you know!"

Fifteen minutes later, Stagg's car arrived in front of The Iron Jim, and he ran inside. Stagg had radioed the station, and another car pulled up with him. Wilkins followed him in.

"Police!" Stagg shouted at an elderly man whose nose was almost flat to his face. "Where's Charlie?"

"Charlie? I dunno," the man shouted back.

"You sure? He was here a minute ago, wasn't he? Where's he gone?" Stagg tried to hide the desperation in his voice.

"I don't know, I tell you. He said he had some business to finish off."

"What sort of business? Where did he go?"

"I don't know, I tell you. He said he wouldn't be long, and that was ages ago. That's all I know. Honest!"

"What car does he drive? Come on, man, it's urgent!"

The man paused until he saw Stagg's steely eyes glittering. He shrugged his shoulders.

"I think it's a white Cortina Estate."

Stagg told Wilkins to stay at the gym until he received further instructions. He tore out of the building, jumped in his car and started driving down the nearby streets. He alerted officers on the radio to keep a lookout for a white Cortina Estate. After a couple of minutes, the radio reported that one had been spotted in the Saxon Street area across town. As it was the only report, Stagg drove there as fast as he could.

CHAPTER 17

Hudson opened her eyes. Someone was in the room with her, and she could hear them scuttling about. She closed her eyes again and opened them to see her new 'friend'. He was opening and closing the cupboard drawers, stuffing anything he found into a paper carrier bag. He looked edgy, and she suspected her cover was blown.

Hudson squinted at him through her lashes, pretending to be asleep. Her head felt a bit clearer today, and the thunder in her ears had died down. Her stomach lurched as she saw Charley Brooks pick up a pillow and approach the bed. He sat on the bed beside her. She pretended to wake up, stretched, and did her very best smile. "Oh, hello! God, that was some strong stuff you gave me, wasn't it? Have you got any more?" Charley wasn't smiling, and Hudson boldly tugged at the pillow in his hands. "Oh! Is this for me? How kind." She smiled again.

Charley leaned forward and whispered in her ear, "Yes, it is for you, darling. Now, what am I going to get in return?" He released the pillow and placed his hand on her thigh before trying to force himself on top of her.

"No, no!" Hudson shouted. She felt sick as she started to stroke his greasy hair. "No, no! Not like this, not with you! I want it to be nice!"

Charley lifted himself up and narrowed his eyes. He hesitated, sat up, and reached into his pocket. Hudson stiffened, but he got out a cigarette, lit it, took a drag and stood up.

Hudson took a deep breath, straightened herself up a little and pulled her skirt down. The man watched her and chuckled but said nothing. He shook his head. Hudson wasn't sure if her cover was blown or not. She felt a lot more awake today and noticed he'd left his carrier bag near the bed, but it was just out of reach.

The man finished his cigarette. "You know, me and you could have had a great thing going. But no. You've spoilt it, haven't you?"

"How have I spoilt it?" Hudson sat up. "I've been sleeping!" The man gripped the end of the bedstead.

"Cos you're a bloody copper, that's why, and I hate coppers!"

Hudson took a deep breath as he stepped forward. "And I like bad boys!" she snapped. "That's why I joined the force. I wanted excitement. That's why you caught my eye. God, those chaps at the station are all wimps. Especially that Stagg. I need a real man, someone who knows his own mind, someone like you!"

She hoped above hope that he'd swallow her bluff and did her best to give him a seductive look. She really wished the 'wimp' Stagg was with her now instead of this horrible thin man.

Charley knew there were crooked policemen, but not crooked policewomen. He would be crazy to believe her, and it went against all his instincts. But maybe, just maybe, she was telling the truth. He wanted to believe it because he wanted her.

She was a beauty with her long, jet-black hair. What his grandad would have called 'a buxom girl', not like that skinny Jenny. He knew he'd have no trouble finding customers for this woman. But no, she was too good for that. No, maybe he could use her to his advantage, with her being in the police as well, and he intended to have some fun finding out. He stubbed his cigarette out and then lit another. He needed to think.

Hudson moved upright on the bed. If she could grab the bag, maybe she could hit him with it and escape. She was poised, ready, in case he decided to attack her. He seemed to be thinking about what she'd said.

Bravely, she stuffed the pillow he had dropped on the bed, put it around her back and said, "I don't suppose you've fetched me anything to eat, have you? I could eat a horse. Or fish and chips. Well, I prefer potato scallops, do you?"

The man said nothing and approached the bed. He picked up the bag and put it near the door. Then he sat down and ran his hand along her leg.

"Fish and chips are too good for you, darling. I have something else in mind for you. Come here."

***

That night, Hudson felt her body being clawed at. There was a whirring noise in her ears, and all she could see were bright-coloured lights floating in the air. Someone, somewhere, was talking gibberish to her, and she couldn't see or understand them. She put her hands over her ears and managed to sleep for a while. Something woke her up suddenly. She was thirsty, and her throat felt as if it was on fire. She stretched her eyelids open and tried to focus her blurred vision. The bright lights had thankfully gone. Then she saw them. A huge one and a skinny one, and they were chattering away like monkeys do. Hudson grasped her hands to her chest as the big monkey came towards her, and she cowered into a corner.

The big monkey took a swipe at her. She felt the blow of his large hand against her face, and she banged her head. She looked around, her eyes wide with fear, and saw some tall white trees nearby. Desperate, she tried to climb up them, but they were cold and smooth, as they were made of iron. She was lying on a ledge at the top of a high cliff. There was no escape. She screamed, but there was no sound. The beast approached.

Suddenly, the little monkey distracted the big one and chattered in his face, pulling him away. The big monkey carried on staring at her, grinning. Hudson pressed herself as hard as she could into the corner and kicked her feet out at the big monkey as he came back towards her, touching her legs. She felt her skin burn as he grabbed her ankles, pulling on her legs, twisting them cruelly. She thought he was going to throw her off the cliff, but he just laughed in her face as tears rolled down her cheeks. The other monkey screamed in his ear, and the big one dropped her as if she were a stick. Then they both went over to the other side of the ledge, chattering quietly.

Hudson curled up in a ball, pulling herself back into the corner, away from the cliffside. She was terrified when the two monkeys sat down across from her and started smoking some cigarettes. Hudson rubbed her eyes, incredulous, and they laughed at her. Her vision cleared a little, so she could finally see, and then she fainted.

CHAPTER 18

Stagg's search of the disused buildings at Saxon Street had revealed nothing other than a thin blanket on an old iron bedstead. If Hudson had been detained there, there was no trace of her now and no trace of a white Cortina or Charley Brooks. He had already set up a discreet search for Hudson, as he didn't want it reaching the papers, not yet, but he knew it would only be a matter of time before the news broke.

After a few minutes, Stagg decided to head down to Charley Brooks's house. He radioed Wilkins to meet him at the Links. There was a slim chance that Hudson could be there, but Stagg knew he was grasping at straws. Stagg and Wilkins arrived at Charley Brooks's house at the same time.

"Anything?" Stagg said to Wilkins.

"No sir. Sorry, sir."

"Right. Let's see what Mrs Brooks has to say, shall we?"

They knocked on the door, and Jan Brooks answered it.

"Oh, what do you want? I can do you for victimisation, coming round here. It's harassment, you know!" She glared at the two officers.

"Is your husband in, Mrs Brooks? I'd like a word with him, please," Stagg asked.

"No, he isn't, not that it's anything to do with you. He's out on business, if you must know. Now clear off!"

She tried to slam the door, but Stagg had his foot in the way. He pulled Hudson's photo out of his pocket and pushed the photo under her nose. "Do you recognise this woman?"

"What woman?"

"This one," Stagg snarled.

She glanced at the photo. "No, I haven't seen her. Why?"

"We think your husband may know her," Stagg said, watching for a reaction.

"What? My Charley? Why would he know her? What do you mean? Let's have another look!" She squinted at the picture.

"Yeh, maybe I have. Has she been to The White Lion lately? These sorts of girls seem to follow my Charley round, you know. Gold diggers they are and all. After his money, they are."

"How does he earn his money, Mrs Brooks? It's a lovely house you have here," Stagg added.

"You mind your own business," she snapped.

"Any idea where your husband could be, Mrs Brooks?" asked Wilkins.

"No, I don't know, I told you. Now clear off, both of you, before I report you." This time she slammed the door shut.

"Come on, Wilkins. Let's go back to the station. We need to make sure that they've put out an alert for Brooks's car."

"Yes, sir. I'll follow you back."

Once Stagg had confirmed the radio alert had been put out, he and Wilkins drove up to Whytfield Hall.

It was a large manor house which had several outbuildings. Stagg had played in the estate's woods as a boy, so he knew the area well.

As they drove to Whytfield Hall, Wilkins said, "I'm sorry that Hudson's gone missing, sir. I hope nothing bad has happened to her. She's been very helpful to me since I arrived at the station. And she's not stern at all like I first thought!"

Stagg's hands gripped the wheel. "No, not stern at all, Wilkins."

"Sir? I know that my uncle, the chief, has sort of pushed me to work with you, and I'm truly sorry about that. I was never sure I wanted to get into police work, and you know what mothers are like." Stagg nodded but said nothing. His own mother was such a gentle soul. "Well, anyway, I just wanted to thank you, sir, for being patient with me. I'm glad I wasn't put with Burns, sir."

"Burns is your commanding officer, Wilkins. Are you enjoying the work?"

"Not now, because of what's happened to Hudson. But yes, I am, sir."

"Good! Here we are." Stagg turned into Whytfield Hall's drive and pulled up in front of the wide entrance.

The door was answered by an elderly butler. "Yes?" he boomed.

"Hello, I'm Inspector Stagg from Whytfield police. We'd like permission to search your outbuildings, as someone has gone missing."

"Come in. I'll ask Lord Whytfield if he can see you. Please wait here."

The butler marched off down a passage that was lined with oak panelling. A grand staircase led upstairs.

"This is a big place, isn't it, sir?" Wilkins whispered.

"Yes, very grand, Wilkins."

The butler returned and ushered them into a study. A thin man sat behind a very large desk. He stood up when the two officers entered.

"Good afternoon, gentlemen. How can I help you?"

"Hello. I'm Inspector Stagg, Lord Whytfield. We'd like permission to search your outbuildings, sir, as a woman has gone missing."

"Oh, dear. Yes, certainly. Search away, and let's hope you find her."

"Thank you, sir."

"And we'll keep a lookout for anyone hanging about, won't we, Jenkins?"

"Yes, of course."

The butler ushered them downstairs, through the kitchen, and directed them towards the sheds and stables that skirted the Hall's rear yard. Stagg and Wilkins went through them all, moving boxes and crates and peeping into old cupboards and ancient horse-drawn coaches. But their search revealed nothing. They thanked the butler and returned to the station.

The two police officers stayed at the station until late in case there were any further sightings of a white Cortina. Stagg sent Wilkins home at six o'clock, but by eight o'clock, Stagg decided to call it a day but made sure that the night team would alert him at home if there were any developments. He was surprised to see Wilkins in the car park.

"I thought I'd have a bit of a drive around, sir. You know, just in case."

"Great minds think alike, Wilkins! Where are you going to? Over to the east side of town? I'll cover the Links side and up by the lake. We'll meet in about an hour, by the bus station. Good!"

Stagg got in his car and sped off while Wilkins turned out of the yard in the opposite direction. Stagg drove around and went up to the lake where he and Hudson had enjoyed their fish and chip supper.

He switched off the engine and ran his fingers through his hair. "Where on earth could she be?" he thought, racking his brains. He dared to hope that she was still alive. The chief was waiting in Stagg's office when they returned.

"Well? Any news on Hudson?"

"No, sir. But we have a lead, and it could involve Charley Brooks. We have put out an alert to establish the whereabouts of his car."

"Brooks? Are you sure? After the last fiasco?"

"Positive, sir. We visited his house, but he wasn't there. I'll call back there later."

"Well, tread carefully, Stagg. Very carefully! We don't want anything happening to Hudson. She's a good WPC. Now get on."

He left the office, and Stagg muttered, "I know she's a good WPC. I know."

Stagg had slept very little that night and had spent it at the station. There was still no news on Charley Brooks's whereabouts or, more importantly, Hudson's.

The chief had decided not to place Brooks's house under police surveillance for fear of 'victimisation', much to Stagg's disgust.

Stagg was making himself a strong black coffee the next morning when WPC Jones rushed up to him. Stagg's heart sank.

"Sir, there's been a murder on the Links! It's Charley Brooks, sir!" Relief soared through Stagg as he jumped up. He'd thought it was Hudson.

"Charley Brooks? I'd better get across there now. Usual procedure, Jones, alert the coroner. Where's Wilkins? Ah! There you are. Come on." Wilkins, who'd just arrived at work, trotted out after Stagg and got into his car.

"Charley Brooks is dead. But if he's dead, sir, how will we find Hudson?"

"Wilkins! Don't worry about that. We'll find Hudson."

"I know, sir, but time's going on….'

"Yes, Wilkins, I do know! Now just shut up, and let's try and sort this mess out, shall we?" Stagg gripped his fingers tightly on the steering wheel.

"Yes, sir."

At Charley Brooks's house, a police car was parked outside, and a policeman stood by the front door. The pathologist was there already. They passed the policeman and entered a smart hallway full of paintings and large vases. They walked to the dining room, where a small, thin man lay slumped over the table. Yardley, the pathologist, was examining the victim's head, and he looked up.

"Ah, Stagg. Hello."

Stagg nodded. "What is it, George? Suicide?"

"Good god, no! He's been poisoned. My tests will confirm later. Don't touch anything on the table. I think it was cyanide. It looks like it was in one of these letters delivered today."

"Someone posted him cyanide. Good God!"

"Looks like it. Carefully done, mind you. It was double wrapped, and the package stated that it was only for the victim."

"I see. Still a big risk, though, if the package had split open."

"Yes, indeed. Let me show you...." Yardley carefully pulled out a large envelope from under the dead man's hand. A trail of white powder had spilled out of a small but thick polythene bag. Wilkins stepped forward to get a better look. "Careful! You won't want to breathe in this stuff." Wilkins stepped back.

"Any note with it, George?" Stagg ventured.

"Yes, but you'll have to give me a bit more time to get it cleaned up for you. This stuff is dangerous, you know!" Yardley held the envelope with tweezers and teased it into a bag.

"Yes of course. Could you just show it to me, then? I won't touch it." Stagg nodded.

"Oh, very well. Here, see, it says something like *'Charley. This is some good stuff. I can get some more ready for delivery if you like. I'll telephone you tonight at six. Fred.'* It could be anybody."

"Yes. *'Telephone you tonight.'* Hmm." Stagg pondered a moment.

"It was carefully wrapped up. A thick envelope, then inside two polythene bags."

"So, it was definitely aimed at Charley Brooks? No one else?"

"Yes. It's clearly marked, see—*'to be opened ONLY by C Brooks.'* But they still took a risk."

"Yes, they did. Thank you."

"You're welcome, Stagg. Any news on the WPC yet?" Yardley carefully placed the letter, envelopes, and the powder package into a specimen bag.

"No, not yet. Let me know when the area is clear, George. Come on, Wilkins. We'd better have a word with Mrs Brooks."

They heard Mrs Brooks before they saw her. She was wailing like a banshee, crying out, "My Charley!" every few seconds. When she saw Stagg and Wilkins, she screamed, "I bet this has got something to do with you lot! Coming here making accusations! Well, my Charley's dead now, so what are you going to do about that, eh?" She buried her face into some tissues and started to sob again.

Stagg said, "I'm very sorry to hear about your husband, Mrs Brooks. Could I just ask you to tell me what exactly happened here this morning?"

A plain, stout woman, who had her arm around her, said, "Don't you answer no questions, Jan, unless you're up to it! These police can wait a minute or two, surely?" She glared at Stagg, who ignored her and waited.

"It's all right, Joan. I'm not afraid of any policeman. Besides, I've met them before." Mrs Brooks blew her nose loudly into a handkerchief. She looked at Stagg and Wilkins, then she sat up a little and leant forward. "You'd better find out who did this to him. You better had!"

"Yes, we'll try our best," said Stagg.

"Good! Well, he'd just opened some letters. He was drinking his coffee because he'd come in late last night. He usually drinks tea in the morning."

"Do you know where he'd been, Mrs Brooks?"

"No, I don't. Business, he'd said. Anyway, like I said, he was late getting in, so he drank his coffee quickly to wake himself up a bit. Then he opened his letters."

"Did he say where they were from?"

"Yes, one was an electric bill for the gym—he was angry about that, as he said it was too much, and he would phone them later about it. Only he won't be doing that now, will he?" She started to cry again. Stagg waited till she calmed herself a little.

"And the other letters?"

"Oh! There was one from the council about something and one from Baines. Then this thick one. It had something wrapped up in it. Wrapped up tight, it was. Charley was cursing, trying to open it. Said it was like a pass-the-parcel!"

"What happened when Mr Brooks had opened his letters?"

"I don't know! I was eating my cereal. Charley must have opened it. I don't know what was in it, but Charley came over all queer all of a sudden! Then he just let out a bit of a scream, and…and….' She collapsed back onto the settee, and Stagg knew there could be no more questions about Charley. He got up.

"Thank you, Mrs Brooks, for helping me, at this sad time. There's just one more thing, if I may ask. Did your husband own any other property other than the gym in the area?" Mrs Brooks rubbed her eyes and shook her head before burying her face in her hands.

Stagg went through to the dining room and asked the pathologist when he'd have his report.

"Soon as I've done it, Stagg."

As they were leaving, a policeman opened the garage door. Inside stood a white Cortina.

"Look, sir!" Wilkins said.

"Indeed!" said Stagg.

"But isn't that the car we were looking for last night?"

"Yes, it is. But our question now should be who killed Charley Brooks? And why?"

"Perhaps it was his brother. The other chap Mrs Morris told us about."

"Maybe. Maybe not. Let's look at the car. See if you can get the keys from the house."

On Wilkins' return, Stagg looked through the windows and carefully opened the door.

"We should wait till it's been dusted, really, Wilkins. I can't see very much in here. Just a minute, what's this?" He lifted out a carrier bag from the corner of the boot. It contained a glass and a half-empty bottle of clear liquid. "Here! Give this to the pathologist to analyse. It could be important. And ask them to dust this glass, Wilkins! Careful now!"

Underneath the bag was a flimsy blanket. On close examination, Stagg could see long, dark hairs on it and was convinced that they were Hudson's. There were also some fish and chip wrappers. He scrutinised the rest of the vehicle but could see nothing else of interest. They left the keys with one of the policemen for the pathologist and returned to the station.

***

Stagg had just entered his office when the phone rang. He knew who it would be.

"Stagg? What are you doing about this death on the Links? Shocking for that area, isn't it?"

"Indeed, sir. It's shocking for everyone." Stagg knew that the chief lived on the Links estate.

"No leads as yet, I suppose?"

"None yet, sir, but I'll keep you informed."

"Good! Make sure you do. And nothing on Hudson yet?"

"No, sir, not yet."

Stagg shook his head. *Any murder is shocking,* he thought. He met Burns in the corridor.

"Well, Stagg? Anything I can do to help?"

"No, sir, thank you."

"You're sure? And no news of the WPC's whereabouts?"

"No, sir."

"Okay. Let's hope we find her soon."

"Sir!" That was Stagg's constant hope. Burns wandered back to his own office, and Stagg called his assistant.

"Right, Wilkins. I want you to visit the chip shops in town and see if they remember someone in a white Cortina last night."

"Chip shops, sir?" Wilkins asked.

"Yes, Wilkins. Off you go. And get times if any of them do remember. Anything at all."

Wilkins knew better than to question Stagg's motives, so he pulled his coat on and left.

The pathologists were quick to produce their report. It stated that there were three sets of fingerprints on the car, those of Charley Brooks, plus two other sets of fingerprints. Stagg knew it would probably be his brother's and asked them to run a check on Bobby Brooks. It was a match. The other set was smudged, so were more difficult to match.

When Wilkins returned, he said there had been a collection of chips the previous night at Wenbury Road Chip Shop.

"A white car, but the shopkeeper couldn't swear it was a white Cortina. But it was late on, about ten o'clock. They'd just been on the point of closing, sir."

"Any description?" Stagg asked.

"Yes, sir. That's the thing. It was a thin chap, he said. He bought two fish. The shopkeeper was annoyed because he'd just given the last of the chips to some gipsy children—it saves them going to waste. He had to make them quick, and he said it was the last thing he wanted to do because he was just going to close for the night. Was it Charley Brooks, sir? It must be, mustn't it?" Wilkins smiled in excitement.

"We can't be sure. Wilkins. We don't want to make any false accusations.'"

"No, sir. It's a shame, though. It must have been him, I'm sure."

"Maybe, Wilkins."

"Anyway, the chip shop owner was annoyed with whoever it was."

Stagg grabbed a notebook from his pocket and quickly flicked through the pages. Wilkins hadn't noticed that Stagg kept notes before, but it didn't surprise him, really. Stagg quickly dialled a number.

"Mrs Brooks? Mrs Jan Brooks? It's Inspector Stagg here. I'm sorry to bother you, but I just wondered whether your husband brought home fish and chips last night for supper...No, I'm not joking…He didn't? That's all I need to know…Thank you…No, no further information yet, sorry. I'll let you know as soon as I have some. Goodbye."

Stagg replaced the receiver. "Let's head over to Bobby Brooks's house, Wilkins."

***

The street where Bobby Brooks lived was untidy, and Wilkins noticed that many of the gardens were unkempt.

"This is a bit different to his brother's house, isn't it, sir? Like chalk and cheese if you ask me."

"Yes, Wilkins." Stagg nodded.

They knocked on the door, and Bobby Brooks opened it.

"Yes? What do you want?" he snarled, drawing the door to a close at the back of him.

Stagg said, "We want to talk to you about your brother. Can we come in, Mr Brooks?"

"No! Tell me here. I don't want you lot in my house!"

"Very well, then, Mr Brooks. I didn't want to tell you on the doorstep, but I'm afraid your brother is dead."

The big man gasped and placed a huge hand on his chest, his mouth falling open, showing gaps in his gums where teeth had once been. "What? Our Charley? Never! You're having a laugh!"

"I'm sorry, but it's true. May we come in?" Stagg persisted.

"Please yourself!"

The man left the door open and went back inside. They followed him into a dingy hallway, where a coat rack was crammed with coats. They walked through into a back room where a rank smell of stale cigarette smoke hit them. There were pots in the sink, dirty cups on the table, along with a half empty bottle of milk. The big man sat down and pushed his hand over his head.

"Charley's dead? I don't believe it! You sure this isn't one of your tricks?" he snarled.

"Tricks? What tricks are those, Mr Brooks?"

"To get me to talk, that's what."

"Talk? Talk about what?"

Bobby Brooks jumped up, scattering the chair backwards onto the dirty lino. "I dunno! What do you want here anyway? Victimisation, that's what it is. That's what Charley says. You'd better get out, both of you. Trying to frighten me, are you, coming here? Well, you don't frighten me. Nobody does!"

"All right, Mr Brooks, calm down. We just thought we'd let you know. Sorry to be the bearer of bad news." Stagg moved to the door.

"Sorry? You ain't sorry! Your lot are never sorry! Look how our dad ended up. That was all the police's fault, Charley says."

"Do you know anything about a girl Charley had met?"

Bobby Brooks picked up the chair and sat down. "Girl? What girl? Charley was married."

"Are you married, Mr Brooks?"

"Me? No. I live here with my mum. She looks after me well enough."

"Do you like girls?" Stagg persisted.

"Course I do. 'Ere, what are you saying? I'm no queer, you know!" he spat, glaring at Stagg.

"No, of course you're not, Mr Brooks." Stagg held his gaze, then turned his back on him. "I don't suppose you go to the chip shop on Wenbury Road, do you? Only I've heard that they're going to close, have you?"

"What are you going on about? The chip shop?" Bobby Brooks chuckled at the policeman and wondered how he had got to be an inspector. Even Wilkins looked surprised.

"I just thought you might know, that's all," Stagg persisted.

"Get out! You come here, tell me my brother's dead, call me a queer, and now you're going on about a chip shop." Brooks stood up. He was tall and heavy, but Stagg matched him in height. Stagg's steely eyes didn't flinch and pierced Bobby Brooks's watery gaze. Wilkins straightened himself up, ready for action and alert. Brooks moved away from Stagg towards the window and clenched his fists.

"Yes, sorry about that. It was a bit insensitive of me. But I do enjoy the fish from there, don't you? Sorry, Mr Brooks," Stagg simpered, while Wilkins, who could hardly believe his ears, said nothing.

"Well, that's more like it. I am Mr Brooks, and for your information, no, I haven't had anything from that chip shop for ages." He relaxed his fists, sat down again, and rested his muscular arms on the table, looking down.

"But now Charley's gone. I'm going to miss him. My little brother!"

"I'm sure you will. If you think of anyone who may have wanted to harm him, then you can get in touch with me at the station, Mr Brooks." Stagg moved towards the kitchen door that was blackened by dirty handprints.

The big man's shoulders moved up and down, and at first, Stagg thought he was upset, but when he turned around towards them, he could see that he was laughing. "Get in touch with you lot. You must be joking! I bet it was you lot that sorted Charley out. Yes, I bet it was! He said you weren't going to let him get away with it. But we'll get the upper hand in the end, don't you worry."

"What do you mean by that? All we've done is inform you of your brother's sudden death." Stagg stayed where he was. The big man leaned back against the sink and folded his arms.

"I ain't telling you lot anything. Now clear off from here!" he yelled.

As Stagg and Wilkins left, they passed a red Cortina parked around the corner.

"Look, sir!" Wilkins said, pointing.

"Yes, Wilkins. I see it. We'll get someone to check it out from the station. We'd better get back in case anything comes in about Hudson."

"Of course." Wilkins paused, then smiled. "All this talk about chips has made me a bit hungry."

"Yes, well, food is the last thing on my mind, Wilkins."

"Yes, of course, sir. Mind you. I fancy some of those potato scallops myself. I haven't had any of those for ages."

"Potato scallops?"

"Yes. You know, big rounds of potato dipped in batter and fried. The chip shop owner reminded me about them."

"Why? What did he say?"

"Only that he was so angry last night because he had had to make them special, the scallops, and they take a bit of time to prepare. He wanted to close, you see, sir."

"What? Oh, clever girl! Come on, Wilkins! I know where she is."

CHAPTER 19

When Hudson opened her eyes, she felt cold, and she shivered. A wooden prop held up the ceiling above her. She was in a different place. Across the room, brown cupboards covered one wall, some with their doors missing. A large fireplace was full of ancient cinders, newspapers and a couple of tin cans, and there were two green doors. The barred windows were very tall and dirty, with frosted glazing covered in cobwebs.

Hudson swung her legs over the side of the bench. She pushed her feet against the wooden floorboards and gripped the seat. She eased herself up a little, but her legs were so shaky she decided to stay where she was, for a while at least. She looked at her surroundings, trying to establish where she was. Then she guessed—the old Whytfield Station building, of course.

The Beeching railway cuts had closed the Whytfield Line, but there were still a few semi-derelict buildings in the area. *Perfect place to hide someone*, she thought. She stretched. Her back ached, and so did her legs. She reached down to her feet and felt the soreness of her skin as she rubbed the purple bruises on them. She couldn't see her boots anywhere.

Weird visions of monkeys flooded into her head, and she realised that she had been drugged. She hoped the monkeys wouldn't come back. Her head still felt a bit fuzzy, but she felt okay in general, apart from feeling weak. She took a deep breath and tried to stand again. Her bruised legs shook together violently. She knew the men had hurt her, but her police training overcame any thoughts of self-pity and made her focus on self-preservation.

Hudson stretched her arm out against a wall to steady herself and edged very slowly towards one of the doors. She turned the Bakelite handle, and the door opened to reveal a very dirty toilet and washbasin where a huge spider squatted, flinching with the draught but staying where it was. She had no other choice but to use the toilet and perched on the very edge of the dirty rim. She checked to see if the toilet window could be opened, but it was nailed down and barred. She went back to the other room, closing the door behind her.

She edged towards the other door and tried it. She was unlucky this time; it was locked. Tottering around the room, she checked the cupboards in case they revealed an escape route. All the windows were barred. She sat down on the bench. She needed to think, and she felt tired and hungry. It must be late afternoon, as the light was starting to fade. She pulled the blanket around her and looked at the windows. If she broke one, she might be able to squeeze out between the long bars, but they were quite close together.

Hudson deduced that this must have been the old porter's room, where parcels and freight would have been stored. The bench she was sitting on would have been used regularly by the night porters while waiting for the milk train. The fire grate was quite big, a cooking range with a wide chimney. It would probably have been used to cook simple suppers back in the old days.

Hudson's stomach rumbled loudly, but it cramped into a coiled spring when she heard a car outside. She scrambled back to the corner of the bench and pretended to be asleep. Now she felt better, she hoped for a chance of escape, but she'd need her wits about her. She heard the door opening and held her breath. Slow steps came towards her, and she opened her eyes to see a hand stretching towards her. She sat up quickly.

The man shouted, "Oi! What's your game? Making me jump." He drew his hand back and tried to strike her on the face. Hudson moved quickly out of the way, and he nearly hit the wall.

"You made me jump too!" Hudson shouted back at him. "And I was sleeping as well. Where's Charley, anyway? He said he was going to bring me something nice to eat this morning, and I'm hungry now."

The big man glared at her but then suddenly flopped beside her on the bench, which groaned in protest. His shoulders slouched, and he said, "He's dead! Our Charley's dead!"

Even Hudson was shocked at this news. She heard herself saying, "Dead? Charley? Oh, dear!" She waited a few moments. "Well, what are we going to do now, without Charley? He said he was going to take me places, you know."

"Did he? Well, he ain't here now, so I dunno. I dunno what to do."

"No, I see that. I don't think Charley would have liked it, keeping me locked in here all this time."

The big man jumped up and shouted, "Well, hard luck! I'm not stupid, you know! And I don't need Charley to tell me what to do with you, 'cos I know exactly what I'm doing."

Hudson took a deep breath. "Good! I like a chap who knows his own mind. Shame about Charley, though."

"God, you are a bad 'un, ain't you? Just like Charley said you was." He sat back down next to her, and Hudson did her brightest smile.

"I always try my best." She wondered if the man knew just how hard she was trying.

The big man placed his arm around her. "I knew we'd get on, you and me." He tightened his grip, and Hudson wriggled a little out of it.

"Don't suppose there's any chance of something to eat, is there?"

The big man laughed. "You like your food, you, don't you? I'll nip to the chip shop. I won't be long. I'm a bit peckish myself." He released his grip and left.

Hudson checked the door after he'd gone, but he'd locked it. She checked the windows' bars again to see if any were loose, but they were fixed solid.

This situation needed thinking about, as Stagg would recommend. God, she wished he was here now. He'd know what to do. She stifled a cry from deep within her. If only she'd told him. He must know she's missing by now. Police training unscrambled Hudson's brain. She knew the chip shop wasn't far from the old station, so the brute wouldn't be long. She'd have to keep her wits about her, and she was definitely not going to have anything to drink!

Hudson wondered what had happened to Charley. The hairs on the back of her neck stood up as she pondered whether he'd been killed by his brother. She didn't think so. She almost wished Charley was here, even though he gave her the creeps. His brother was not only unpredictable, but he was also just so big. Hudson knew that she wouldn't be strong enough to fight him off.

She went into the toilet and shouted, "Help! Help!" as loud as she could, but no one heard her. She returned to the bench and slumped down, quite forlorn. No, she'd have to be very careful, very careful indeed. She saw a flash of car lights. He was back.

Bobby Brooks took great care in returning to the old station. He'd driven past it twice before turning in as Charley had shown him. He checked all the time that he wasn't followed. He got out of the car, carrying the chips, and looked around again. There was no sign of any other vehicles.

The light of the day was starting to fade, and the wind whistled through some piles of old machinery and metal that littered the yard. Smiling, he locked his car and tramped through the yard, kicking some old crates in his path. He was hungry and looking forward to having a bit of fun with the girl now that he was in charge, not Charley.

He unlocked the door slowly, cursing as he nearly dropped the bags of chips. He slammed it shut behind him.

"Bloody chips. They nearly fell!"

Hudson jumped when he'd burst into the room, and he plonked himself down heavily next to her. He roughly shoved a newspaper package into her hands.

"Here! They're hot! I'm hungry myself." He tore open his paper package.

"Thanks." Hudson took the package and wondered if he had locked the door. She didn't feel like eating anything, so she nibbled slowly and steadily. She thought she'd try a bit of conversation with the brute.

"These are nice. Did you get them from Wenbury Rd? I like their chips best, don't you?"

"Yes, I do an' all. Not that I'm saying I got them there, mind." He chuckled. "You're not going to catch me out. I'm not as stupid as people think, you know."

"I never said you were stupid, did I? Was that Charley saying that? That wasn't very nice, was it?"

Bobby Brooks snatched her chips and shouted, "Don't you say anything about Charley! He never thought I was stupid. He used to just tease me, that's all. Anyway, you're not having these now! "He threw the papers into the fireplace and finished off his own, staring into space at first until a small smile came on his face.

"Sorry if I upset you, I'm sure. I suppose it was just that Charley was so clever, with the police and everything, you know."

"Huh! We didn't have to worry about the police. Charley had sorted that. What do you know about it, anyway?" Bobby Brooks stretched out his big hand to cup her neck under her chin. Hudson pulled back quickly, but his grip followed her. She knew his powerful hands could probably crush her windpipe as easily as a lollipop stick.

"Nothing! I don't know anything!"

He released his grip on her throat and patted her leg. "Good! 'Cos I wouldn't like to hurt you. Not really. Charley liked you. I don't know why, but…." A sound of glass smashing nearby made them both jump.

The big man sprang up. "Have you been shouting? You bitch!" He tried to hit Hudson, but she dived out of the way and ran to the other side of the room. The sound of another window being smashed reverberated around the building.

"Perhaps it's kids. I haven't been shouting, honest!" Hudson lied.

"I'll give them kids if I get hold of them!"

He stormed out but remembered to lock the door. Hudson grappled with it, but to no avail. She could see that the toilet window had been smashed. She tried to get through the bars, but she was too big. It was dark outside, and all she could see were shadows. She saw the big man in the yard, looking about. He would return soon.

Hudson really feared for her safety now. She looked frantically about the room, and she needed somewhere to hide. It was now or never.

Bobby Brooks could see nothing outside. He circled the yard quickly and disturbed a couple of cats. He stood for a few moments outside the building, scanning the darkness, listening. Satisfied that it must have been kids, he returned inside. He was looking forward to getting friendly with that girl, even though she was a policewoman. He was in charge of things now, not Charley. Things would be done his way for a change.

He unlocked the door. "It must have been kids, after all!" His mouth dropped open when he saw that she had gone.

He ran into the toilet and saw the broken window. Had she really escaped through those bars? He started to ransack the cupboards, slamming the doors, checking to see if she was hiding. He noticed a pile of soot had fallen onto the floor from the chimney, and he smiled.

"Looking for something, Brooks?" A torch flashed in his face.

"Who's that?" Brooks shouted, stepping forward. "Who's that shining a light in my face?"

"Inspector Stagg, Brooks! Now, what are you doing here? I want to know."

"Mind your own business. What are you doing here? This is private property. You got no right to be here. It's ours."

"Yours? You mean Charley's, not yours."

"No! No! Charley said it was ours."

"Charley seems to have told you what he liked. I've checked, and it was registered just in his name. Now, you haven't told me what you're doing here."

The big man sat on the old bench and smiled. "I ain't doing nothing, I told you. Bit of tidying, that's all."

Stagg could see no evidence of this. He picked up the chip papers off the cupboard. "Late supper, was it?"

"Nothing wrong with that. I thought I'd try that chippy you were on about."

He got up, lit the papers in the grate with his lighter and sat down again. "I'm tidying up, see?"

"In the dark, Brooks?"

"No law against that, is there?"

Bobby Brooks sat back down on the bench, smiling as the chip papers, damp with cooking fat and vinegar, shot amber pieces of paper up into the chimney. Stagg had lowered his torch a little to give himself a better view of the room. The papers were starting to throw out a bit of light as they caught fire, and large lumps of soot started to fall from the chimney.

Stagg thought he heard someone cough. He sprang forward and kicked at the fire grate, getting most of the burning papers out from the chimney. His breath was smashed out of his lungs as Brooks rained a couple of blows to Stagg's ribs. Stagg managed to land a few punches to the man's flabby torso before they both fell backwards onto the old bench.

The chip papers, now released from the grate, quickly spread along the thin blanket on the bench. Stagg had fortunately landed on top of Brooks, and he could see Wilkins helping Hudson out of the fire grate.

Stagg felt a crack as Brooks landed another punch to his ribs. He twisted around quickly to avoid another and managed to clamber to his feet. Brooks lunged forward towards him but knocked his head on the wooden prop that was holding the ceiling up. Stunned a little, he stumbled back near the fire. Stagg stepped forward, and Brooks grabbed him, pulling him onto the floor. They both rolled around fighting, each one trying to overcome the other.

The old bench was alight now, and jagged timbers in the walls had started to push out darts of flames that made old advertising posters turn black and curl up. The fire spread to the ceiling, raining down burning chunks of old plasterboard onto the two men. They grappled with each other, Stagg dodging a punch from Brooks, which would have surely broken his jaw. Stagg could feel the heat from the fire through his shoes as he tried to restrain Brooks. He scrambled to his feet and shouted to Brooks, "Come on, man! We've got to get out of here. It's no use fighting."

Brooks pulled himself up from the floor.

"Had enough, have you? You police are all the same. Cowards, you are!"

He started to lunge forward to Stagg again, dodging the wooden ceiling prop, which was now ablaze. He edged around the room, trying to get to the door.

"Wilkins!" Stagg shouted.

Brooks laughed. "You can't catch me out with that old trick. You'll be telling me next that someone's behind me."

Stagg had assumed Brooks had seen Wilkins earlier, but he obviously hadn't. The fire was blazing now, and Stagg could hear the roof timbers cracking with the heat.

"Come on. We've got to get out!" Stagg shouted.

Brooks dived towards him. "No, you're not going anywhere!"

Stagg quickly jumped out of his way, and Brooks landed on his side, knocking himself out.

Wilkins had made sure Hudson was safe outside, and he ran back into the building when he heard Stagg shout. He thought Stagg had everything under control and Brooks would come along quietly. What he actually saw seemed unreal.

Stagg was squatted down, strenuously pulling on Brooks's feet. Brooks looked as if he was out cold. Stagg was surrounded by flames, and large lumps of glowing red wood were dropping on and around him. The small fire had quickly spread through the semi-derelict building, and Stagg was almost surrounded. Wilkins tried to step forward to help him, but it was no use, he was afraid of the fire. He edged his way around the other side.

Stagg shouted, "Can you reach him from there? We've got to get him out!"

A flare of flame roared as more bits of the roof fell. Wilkins swallowed and carefully picked his way through the flames to reach Brooks. He lay unmoving while the fire was lapping around them. Wilkins tried to kick the fire away from them while Stagg was still trying to pull Brooks out by his feet. Wilkins leant down to grab Brooks's arms. Brooks opened his eyes and struck Wilkins with a strong blow. Wilkins fell back onto the fire, and although dazed, instinct kicked in, making him leap forward out of the flames. Brooks had lumbered to his feet, dodging some of the flames that were getting higher.

Stagg jumped up and shouted at Brooks. "Come on, man. You've got to get out of here!"

Brooks saw Stagg's burnt hands and Wilkins' smoking hair, and he smiled, glad they had been hurt after all.

"Come on, Brooks!" Stagg screamed as he heard the roof starting to crack. Wilkins moved back towards the door in case Brooks made a run for it.

There was another huge creaking sound, and a shower of curled orange embers as big as bricks fell on them. Wilkins and Stagg covered their heads with their hands and automatically stepped back. They looked across the flames at Brooks, who held his hands out to them.

"Come on, you lot, help me out of here!" The policemen tried to step forward, but large chunks of blazing timber began falling, making them retreat. "Chicken coppers!" He started laughing and threw back his head as bits of flaming timber crashed down around him.

Stagg and Wilkins grabbed a piece of wood to try to rake out some of the rubbish that was catching fire, but it was no use. They tried again to get near to him, but a sheet of fire barred their way. It was too severe, and the roof had started to collapse. They were sure they could hear him laughing as they ran out of the inferno.

Coughing, they were eager to breathe in the cold, fresh air outside. There was a huge crashing sound as the ceiling caved in, sending a plume of thick, black smoke into the sky.

Hudson was standing by the car door. She ran towards Stagg, into his arms. He cradled her as she softly wept, and he brushed her singed hair. It was finally over.

CHAPTER 20

As Hudson returned home that night, Pamela's mother had been shocked at their black faces and singed hair, but she was so relieved to see her daughter again. Even though they were covered in soot and ash, she showed them into the parlour. Pamela was surprised to see her mum setting out glasses and a half bottle of brandy on the coffee table. They usually only had that at Christmas. Her mum poured them all a good measure and insisted they drink it, which they did. There were a few quiet moments when they all tried to grasp reality.

Hudson and Stagg were sitting together, and Wilkins was in a chair. Hudson was reluctant to leave Stagg's side, enjoying the warmth she could feel coming from him, and he still had a protective arm around her back.

Pamela's mother stood up. "Well, gentlemen, I think this young lady could do with a bath."

"Mum! I'm not a little girl."

Stagg carefully removed his arm. "Your mother's right. You need a rest. You're okay now. You're home." He gently squeezed her arm, and Hudson leaned against him.

"I know. Thank you, and you, too, Wilkins."

Stagg thanked Mrs Hudson for the drinks. She touched his hand to say goodbye, and he winced a little.

"You need to go to the doctors with that. Don't worry about Pam. I'll look after her now."

"Yes, I will. I'll call you in the morning, WPC Hudson. Goodbye."

Later that night, Hudson leant back in the bath, the warmth of the hot water seeping into her body. Another brandy had helped her to warm up, but it did little to quell the coldness that was inside her head. She looked at the bottle of bath salts on the shelf near the bath and the green tiles edged with a black border. She wanted to keep this snapshot in her mind forever. It was safe. She was safe.

Stagg had been so thoughtful and caring tonight. At one point, she thought he was going to kiss her. His steely eyes seemed to see into the depths of her soul, and he had held her tight. She relished that thought as she lay in the warm soapy water.

The following day, Hudson was flicking through a women's magazine. She'd been for a check-up with the police doctor that morning, and he'd taken some blood tests. Other than some bruising, she was unharmed, but he'd quietly recommended that, if needs be, she should do a pregnancy test. The very thought made Hudson feel sick, so she banished it to the back of her mind and didn't mention it to her mother. Mrs Hudson had been fussing around her daughter so much that eventually, Pam had told her to go out to do the daily shopping.

Hudson was glad to be home. The thought of what she'd been through the last few days still made her shudder, but the doctor told her that her mind would blur the memories as time went on. She hoped they were right.

She stretched out on the sofa and nibbled on a chocolate digestive biscuit. She might have another hot bath tonight to help her relax. The doctor didn't know what drugs she'd been given, but any traces should show up in the test samples. He'd told her to take some aspirin if she felt the need. She sighed, trying to relax, and thought of Stagg.

She closed her eyes and drifted off into a dream, seeing Stagg in the distance. Then something dark appeared at the back of him. She couldn't make out what it was at first, then realised it was a big monkey, a gorilla. She woke up with a start, her hands clasped and sweaty. She stood up and paced about for a while. Then she went into the kitchen, got out a duster and window cleaner, and started to clean the windows outside. She needed some fresh air.

***

Wilkins was also glad that things could get back to normal, or as normal as they could be in the police station. He had been so relieved to rescue Hudson but not as relieved as he could see Inspector Stagg was. They all had had black faces, and in another situation, they would have looked quite funny. Even though the fire brigade had arrived quite quickly and hosed the building down, little was left of the old station building.

Wilkins' report had taken some time to write up. He had never liked writing them when he'd been a constable, but he realised now how critical they could be. He remembered how that solicitor had made Mrs Morris's testimony seem unimportant. He regretted that he had viewed her as unreliable and had taken her at face value. No, making assumptions about people was out of order, and the paperwork had to be correct, as Inspector Stagg insisted.

Stagg walked into his office in his usual upright manner. The only indication that he'd been in a fight was a small bandage on one hand and a large plaster on the other. Wilkins waited a few minutes before knocking at his door.

"Sir? I've finished the Brooks report." He stepped inside and placed it on Stagg's desk before sitting down.

Stagg took a few moments to scrutinise it, looking very serious indeed. Then his face broke into a wide smile.

"Excellent, Wilkins! A very good report, and you did a very good job getting Pamela…eh…WPC Hudson out from that chimney. I shall make a note of it in my report. Good police work."

"Thank you, sir. How is Hudson? Is she all right?"

"Good, yes, thank you. I spoke to her mother first thing, and she seemed to have slept well. Of course, she'll be off for a few days, but she's going to be fine. She'll soon be back."

There was a knock at the door, and the chief entered, at which the two policemen jumped up to attention and barked out, “Sir!” at the same time.

“Yes, yes. At ease.” The chief waved his hand and motioned for them to sit. “So glad Hudson’s all right, and all that business is sorted. The Brooks brothers, eh? I wouldn’t have thought they were clever enough to kidnap anyone, though. Is the report finished?”

“Almost, sir. Wilkins has written up his report, and I shall add mine. We should be very grateful to Wilkins, sir. He did some very good police work and was crucial in the rescue of WPC Hudson.”

Wilkins’ eyebrows shot up when he heard this praise from Stagg to his Uncle Brian. He hadn’t really expected Stagg to say anything at all.

The chief beamed at his nephew and shook his hand. “We knew, I mean, I knew that you had the makings of a good policeman. Well done! I take it I can expect both reports sometime this morning, Stagg.”

He glanced at the bandage on his inspector’s hands and said, “Good work,” before slamming the door shut.

Wilkins said, “Thank you, sir.”

“What for, Wilkins? Praise where praise is due. You can make me a cup of tea if you like.”

Stagg chuckled and started on his report. Burns appeared at the door.

"That was a stroke of luck, finding Hudson, wasn't it, Stagg? And the Brooks brothers were behind it all? Who would have thought it, eh?"

"Hudson's safe now, sir."

"That's good. She's a great girl." Burns laughed as Stagg's eyebrows drew together. "Not that you'd notice, Stagg, would you? Too engrossed with your work!" He left before Stagg could reply.

CHAPTER 21

A few days later, on the morning of the Brooks brothers' funerals, Stagg intercepted Wilkins in the police station yard, saying he had decided they would do some surveillance work.

"Where are we going to, sir?" said Wilkins grabbing his overcoat from his car. He'd been hoping for a cup of tea first thing.

"I want to see if anyone goes to Bobby Brooks's house before the funeral."

"Oh yes! Why, sir?" He pulled on his coat.

"Someone may want to check that he hasn't left anything behind."

"Sir?"

"From the robbery at Williams Jewellers, Wilkins."

"Oh, I see!" said Wilkins. But he wasn't sure if he did.

They arrived at the house. Stagg switched off the engine, and they waited a while. He glanced at his watch. It was almost nine o'clock, and there was no sign of anyone. They waited for an hour. Wilkins' stomach rumbled loudly. He'd had no breakfast. He hoped they'd go back to the station soon, but Stagg started up the car.

"We'd better go to the church."

Stagg drove quickly, parking nearby so that they could see the attendees. Several large cars were parked in front of the church already, and Stagg noted some familiar faces amongst the throng of people outside. Most of the women wore stiletto shoes and bright-red lipstick and noisily chattered as they went inside. They reminded Stagg of crows cackling over dead meat.

"They must have been popular," Wilkins said as the funeral hearses arrived.

The coffins were adorned with flowers spelling *'Bobby'* and *'Charley'*. Two black funeral cars followed. Stagg recognised Mrs Brooks, the men's mother—a plain stout woman who wore a small, black hat that was stretched tightly over her head. She wiped her nose quickly with a flowery handkerchief before stuffing it into her bag.

Jan Brooks walked with her, wearing a very tight short skirt and black boots. She wore an enormous floppy hat, and blond curls tried to escape from under its rim. She dabbed her eyes, looking about her. She lit a cigarette, drew a few deep breaths from it, dropped it on the path, placed her booted foot carefully on it and twisted her foot to extinguish it. Then she lifted her head and led the funeral ensemble into the church.

Stagg noticed a couple of press photographers at the church's front gate, so he led Wilkins to a side one. As they opened it, a slim woman dressed in black ran into the church. She did not notice them in her haste. It was Betty from the jewellers.

"Hey, that's Betty. I wonder what she's doing here?" said Wilkins.

Stagg rolled his eyes but simply said, "I wonder?" He'd explain later.

They waited for a couple of minutes, then entered the church and sat at the back near a stone pillar. The organ music played quietly in the cold space, and Stagg scanned the crowd. He had already recognised a couple of local villains and watched Mrs Brooks senior. He could see tears rolling down her cheeks, but her face was wooden. In contrast, Charley's wife sat at the front, sobbing loudly under her large hat. Every now and then, she would glance around at the congregation, almost begging for sympathy and attention. Betty sat by her side, and it was easy to see they were sisters.

Once the coffins appeared, the organ started to play loudly but in a maudlin fashion. As the vicar began the service, Stagg nudged Wilkins to leave. They crept out of the church slowly, but as they came out of the large arched doorway, they bumped into a man in a brown overcoat who was entering the church as quietly as they were leaving it.

"Oh, sorry," he whispered, quickly edging past them.

Stagg simply nodded. When they were outside, Wilkins said, "Well, I didn't see anyone amongst the crowd, did you, sir? I'm not sure who we were looking for, really."

Stagg appreciated his honesty. "Well, you never know till you see it."

They waited outside until the service was over, but Stagg parked around the corner, away from the press. Wilkins popped into the newsagents for something to ward off his hunger until lunchtime, leaving Stagg to enjoy some autumn sunshine. He gazed out of the window at the church. Built out of local stone, it was very pretty, with its elevated position and Norman tower. Stagg had enjoyed many Christmas services there with his mother. He thought it was a shame that it was currently full of most of the town's criminals.

Stagg tapped his fingers on the steering wheel and hoped Wilkins wouldn't be too long. He saw a man pass his car, and it was the same chap he'd bumped into inside the church. He watched him walk down the road and get into a small car. Naturally, Stagg noted down the registration number just to be sure.

Wilkins got back into the car, chewing on a bar of chocolate. He offered Stagg a piece, but he declined. Stagg drove to the old railway station to have a look around. When they arrived, the area had been cordoned off. They stepped over the barrier and walked to the remains of the building. They carefully picked their way through the charred bricks and rubble and made their way towards the remains of the porter's room. The tall window bars were twisted and fused together. Stagg shuddered at the thought of Hudson being imprisoned here. She was lucky to be alive. Wilkins stumbled over at some stones, and a couple of blackened timbers fell.

"Careful!" warned Stagg.

Stagg moved over to where the shelves and cupboards had once stood. Only one remained, its wood blistered, clinging onto a section of wall. He opened the door, and the whole thing fell off. As he jumped out of the way, Stagg noticed the remains of a leather strap under some bricks. Reaching down, he could see it was the remains of a leather bag. He carefully cleared away the bricks to reveal a very dusty pile of jewellery.

"Wilkins! Over here!"

Wilkins clattered over the rubble and saw Stagg pick up a dirty pile of rubbish. When he saw what it was, he said, "Well, I never. You've found it, sir. Here! Use my handkerchief to put it in."

After double-checking the area to make sure they had it all, they returned to the station. Photos of the jewellery were taken for the record before they could be returned to Mr Williams. Most of the dusty pile was intact, but there was some fire damage.

The chief was ecstatic when Stagg informed him of their discovery over the phone. Stagg had thought he had misheard him when he had said, "Excellent work, Stagg!"

Inspector Burns wasn't so complimentary. "Any leads on Charley Brooks's murder, Stagg?"

"No, sir, not yet."

"Ah, well, maybe something will come up, Stagg. You can't get cyanide over the counter, you know."

"No, sir." Stagg's brows furrowed, and Burns sailed out. Before starting his report, he asked WPC Jones to check the registration number he'd noted down at the funeral. He'd set Wilkins the task of checking on Betty's whereabouts. Stagg just needed to confirm something himself, so he phoned the Coroner's Office.

Wilkins had phoned three banks in the town, and he was lucky. On his fourth call to one of the town's building societies, the Shropshire Bank., the manager said, "Yes, I have her excellent references from Williams Jewellers, but she didn't turn up on Monday. Has she been involved in an accident or something?"

"No, sir. It's just a routine enquiry. What was her position going to be, sir?"

"She was going to be a counter clerk, taking and issuing monies. Is she going to start here then?"

"I don't think so, sir. Could you inform us if she makes any further contact with you?"

"Yes, of course. Oh dear, I shall have to choose someone else then. Goodbye."

"Goodbye, sir. Thank you.' Wilkins knew Stagg would be pleased.

Further checks on Betty's employment revealed she had worked at the garage and the Baines factory over the past two years. Betty would have been in a perfect position to provide inside information on building layouts, including monies held in safes.

Stagg and Wilkins were on their way to interview her when a report of a bad car accident came in. Stagg sent Wilkins out to investigate while he went to visit Betty.

Betty Griffiths lived around the corner from Bobby Brooks, but her house was much tidier. Stagg noticed the grass was freshly cut, and tiny white alyssum flowers edged the front path. He knocked on the front door, and Betty opened it.

"Hello, Betty. May I come in? I have a few questions I'd like to ask you if I may."

Betty pulled the door to her. "Questions? What about? I don't work at Williams anymore."

"No, I know. If I could come in?" Stagg stepped forward.

"No, you can't come in."

"All right, then I'm going to have to ask you to accompany me to the station, Betty." Stagg was surprised when she grabbed her coat and slammed the door shut.

"Okay, I'll come to the station. I don't want my mum to know about this." She stomped down the path with her shoulders slouched forward.

At the station, Stagg's interrogation resulted in a full confession from Betty. Charley had given her strict instructions on what to do to get suitable jobs. Once employed, she had passed on the layout of the places to Charley, which provided the two men easy access.

"So, it was you who oiled and unlocked the back gate at Mr Williams' shop?"

Betty sat back in her chair and half smiled. "You know about that, do you? You're not as daft as you look, are you?"

"And was beating up Mr Williams part of your plan, too, so you could get some nice jewellery?"

"No, that wasn't anything to do with me! I didn't know they were going to do that. Really, I didn't! Mr Williams had been very nice to me. Miss Ellis was a bit of an old fusspot, but it was a nice place to work. I asked Charley not to rob him, but he wouldn't have it. But I didn't know they were going to hit him." Betty was breathing hard now.

"So, that's why you were so shocked when we arrived."

"Yes. It was awful. They shouldn't have done that. It was that stupid brother of Charley's."

Betty reached into her bag and got out a packet of cigarettes. She lit one and took a long drag. Then she put the pack back into her bag.

"You were very lucky that Mr Williams wasn't badly hurt, Betty. Very lucky."

"I'm telling you, it was all Charley's idea, not mine. Nothing to do with me!"

"I think you know that isn't true, Betty. You have admitted to being an accessory to at least three robberies, and I'm sure you realise the consequences of that."

"God, you don't mean prison, do you? I told you it was all Charley's ideas, not mine!"

"But Charley's not here, is he?"

"No, he isn't, but don't think I'm taking all the blame. He said I'd get a bit of money and some rings if I did what I was told. That's all it was. You've got to believe me!"

She broke down crying and whispered, "I don't want to go to jail. It was all Charley's fault. I've known him for years since I was small. He always used to bring me sweets when he'd come and see my sister. We used to get up to some tricks! A bit naughty, that's all. I even sneaked into the police station once to pinch a book. I had a big bar of chocolate for that. But I never meant for him to hit Mr Williams like that. It was all getting out of hand."

"When did you steal the book, Betty?"

"Oh, it was about six years ago. Charley was desperate to get that book back. It had all his contacts in it. But lately, he bragged that he was well in with the police. They were turning into right gangsters, like some of the ones they have in the city. I reckon Charley had got some stupid ideas from when he was in Birmingham. He said I had to do what he said, or he'd tell you lot!"

"Did your sister know what he was doing?"

"Our Jan? God no! She's very pretty, but she's a bit dim. Just likes nice things and likes looking nice. No, she thought he was a businessman. Poor cow!"

"And your excellent references?"

"Why, they were easy to fake! There's always plenty of headed paper about everywhere I worked!"

"I see. And what do you know about Mr Baines?"

"Baines? Not much. Charley knew him and asked some questions about him, that's all. Why?"

"Things like when he emptied the safe, I suppose?"

"I won't go to prison for this, will I? I mean, it wasn't me doing the robberies, was it?" Betty pleaded.

"I can't say for sure. I'm sure the judge will consider your awkward position related to the family, et cetera. It will be better for you, especially now, if you tell us the truth. Especially your relationship with Charley Brooks from the start, Betty. It would be a great help." He nodded to WPC Jones, who was also in the interview room. "Now, Betty, WPC Jones will make you a cup of tea. You'll have to stay here for a while. I'll see you before you go home. You'll need to sign your statement. I don't know what the result will be, but hopefully, it won't be too harsh. I'll see you later."

Betty got up, and by the door, she turned to Stagg.

"If you see Mr Williams and Miss Ellis, tell them I'm sorry he was hurt. They were both very nice to me. You will tell him that, won't you?"

"Yes, Betty, I'll tell him."

Stagg sighed and looked down at his notes. He knew he had another report to write and type up, but before he started, he made a couple of phone calls. After he'd read Betty's statement, he decided to pursue his enquiries further. He'd planned to see Hudson that night but had to check something out first.

He phoned Hudson's house, and his stomach churned when he heard her say, "Oh, so you're not coming tonight? I see, Adam. I'll see you tomorrow night, then, will I?"

"Sorry, of course, you will, Pam. I just need to check this out. It's work. Sorry, Pam."

Stagg didn't return home until almost midnight and went straight to bed, but he couldn't sleep for ages. He needed to get things straight in his mind.

CHAPTER 22

The following day, Stagg had the results of the registration check. It confirmed, as he knew, that the car belonged to Harold Jones. Wilkins was still busy following up on the car accident and some car thefts at a local garage.

Stagg drove to Monkton and went into the local shop. The shopkeeper was a busty woman in her mid-forties. Stagg looked through some magazines that were in a rack by the door.

"You all right there?" she enquired, leaning on the worn wooden counter.

"Yes, thank you, just looking."

Stagg stepped forward and looked at the chocolate bars under the glass on the counter. He eventually decided on a bar of Fry's plain chocolate.

"I'll take this, please. It was my Nana's favourite."

"Oh, yes, funny that. My Gran used to like it too." The woman stood up a little and briefly touched her hair. She gave Stagg his change. "You're new to the area, aren't you, sir?"

"Yes, just trying to find an old friend of the family. Maybe you know him? Harold Jones?" He put the bar of chocolate in his pocket. He'd give it to Wilkins later.

"Oh, yes, everyone who's been to school here knows Harold. Lovely man. He's the school caretaker. Lives just up the road. Straight up on the right, number forty. You can't miss it."

The bell tinkled, and another customer entered the shop. Stagg took the opportunity to leave, but he could feel the shopkeeper's eyes on him. He drove up the road and parked outside number forty. He waited a few minutes to collect his thoughts and knocked on the door. Harold opened it and was drying his hands on a tea towel.

"Yes? What is it? Oh, it's you. Hello."

"Hello, Mr Jones. I'm just doing some routine checks in the area, sir, about car thefts. I wonder if I can come in for a couple of minutes?"

"Oh! Well, I suppose so. I was just making my lunch." A smell of burning toast came from inside the house, and he dashed back into the kitchen. "Oh, darn it! I've burnt my toast. Sorry, please come in and take a seat." He fished out two charred pieces of bread from under the gas grill and threw them into the waste bin. He sat down at the table. "Would you like a cup of tea?"

"No, thank you, sir. I just wondered whether you had noticed any of these cars at the school. You work there, I believe?"

Stagg handed an old list of car details to Harold, who immediately put on his glasses. Stagg looked around the sitting room. There were clothes over some of the dining chairs, washed clothes that were drying over a wooden clothes maid, and some pots in the sink, but it was clean, just a bit untidy.

"Yes, that's right. No, sorry, I don't think I've seen any of these." Harold put down his glasses and asked, "How did you know I worked at the school?"

Stagg smiled. "Oh, you know what the police are like. There's not much that we don't know."

"I don't know about that," Harold huffed.

"Oh? Why do you say that, Mr Jones? Have you had any problems with the police?"

The man chuckled. "No, not anymore. It was only when Jenny went missing, you know?"

"Oh, I see." Stagg carefully folded up the list.

Harold Jones stood up. "Is there anything else, only I have to get back to work? The classrooms won't clean themselves, you know." He smiled at Stagg, but his eyes were serious.

"Mr Jones, I know you were at Charley Brooks's funeral. Why was that?"

Harold picked up the tea towel and rubbed some plates dry before putting them in the cupboard.

"No law against it, is there?"

"No, sir. I just wondered how you knew him, that's all."

"Well, it doesn't matter now that he's dead. He was the chap that our Jennifer had taken up with, in his big car. It was him."

"Charley Brooks? You're sure? How did you find out?"

"I saw his picture in the paper. It was definitely him. And that court case was chucked out. A fiddle if you ask me. Bloody rogues! They never get what they deserve, do they? I wanted to make sure it was him. I'm glad he's dead. I really am!"

"I'm sure you are, Mr Jones. Can I just ask, do you use any cyanide in your job at all?"

"Yes, I do. You have to be very careful with it, I know."

"What do you use it for?"

"I get it from the Education Department for wasps' nests. We have them sometimes in the school, you see."

"Do you have any at the moment?"

"Yes, it's locked up in the shed. I can show you if you like."

"No, that's all right, sir. But if you can continue to keep it safe, for the moment."

"Yes, of course, I will. Why are you asking? 'Ere, I hope you don't think I killed that chap, 'cos I didn't. He's caused me enough misery as it is."

"No, sir. I'll be in touch if I need any more information."

"Like what?"

"It's just so I can eliminate you from our enquiries. That's all."

"Good! Well, I didn't kill him, even though I felt like it, after what he did to my Jenny and then Beryl. He was just a scumbag! He got his just desserts, that's all I can say, and good riddance!"

"I wouldn't say that too often, Mr Jones, or someone might believe that you did kill him. Goodbye." As Stagg went to the door, he noticed some family photos on the sideboard. "Nice pictures. My mum used to have a hat just like that."

"That's my wife before she was poorly."

Stagg picked up another photo of a young girl. "So, this is your daughter, Jennifer?"

"Yes, it is. Well, goodbye."

Stagg carefully placed the photo back down on the sideboard and left. He knew he should really get Mr Jones down to the station to make a formal statement, as he did have a very strong motive for killing Charley Brooks, but Stagg just couldn't believe him to be a murderer. For once, Stagg wasn't going to follow procedure. He'd make a record of his findings once he was back at his desk.

***

On his way back to the station, he visited Mr Baines at the factory.

"Well, Stagg? Any more information about my money?"

"No, sir, I'm afraid not. Do you know a Mr Charles Brooks?"

"Charles Brooks? Oh, Charley Brooks, do you mean? Yes, he was in school with me. Why?"

"He's dead."

"Dead? Oh."

"When did you last see him, Mr Baines?"

"Charley? I haven't seen him for years. Why?"

"He was poisoned, Mr Baines."

"Poisoned? Are you sure?"

"Yes. You seem surprised, Mr Baines."

"Well, I'm shocked, of course, but poisoned! I thought it might have been...."

"Yes? What did you think it could have been? Drugs?"

"I don't know. One hears rumours."

"And you haven't seen him recently?"

"No, I told you!"

"Even though he's been seen coming here on a monthly basis. What was the reason for that, Mr Baines?"

"I don't know where you've got your information from, Stagg, but you're wrong!"

"I see. Do you use any cyanide on site, Mr Baines? For pest control?"

"Yes, I think we do for wasps' nests. The store's chap will be able to tell you. Why? You surely don't think I had anything to do with Charley's death, do you? Because if that's what you're saying, I'll report you to Burns!"

"I'm not saying that at all. Mr Baines. Can you direct me to your stores?"

"I'll show you myself! Come along."

They made their way through the factory, down some stairs and across the factory floor. Stagg caught sight of some of the men he'd previously spoken to, but they all kept their heads down as Mr Baines passed. They entered a small room which smelt of lubricating oil and metal. An elderly man with glasses greeted them.

"Hello, Mr Baines! What can I do for you, sir?"

"Now, Wilson! Show Inspector Stagg here the cyanide we keep for the wasps' nests."

"Of course, it's on the top shelf here. Just a minute, sir."

He wrestled with a wooden step ladder and plonked it in front of a set of shelves. He stretched up into a dark corner and pulled out an old OXO tin. He stepped down the ladder slowly.

"Here it is, sir. Just a minute, I'll get you some plastic gloves."

When Baines had put the gloves on, he carefully opened the tin. His eyes widened, and he spun the box around to the storekeeper.

"Where is it, then, Bert? What have you done with it?"

The storeman looked uncomfortable. "I'm sure there was some left, sir. We only did the nest a few months back, and there was definitely some left!"

Stagg asked, "Who else knows where this is stored?" He closed the tin.

"Most of the lads do. They all help putting it in the nests. But we're always very careful, sir."

"I'm sure you are. Thank you. I'll take the box with me if you don't mind putting it in a bag. Thank you. That will be all for now, Mr Baines. Goodbye."

***

When Stagg returned to the station, Wilkins was looking at some lists and making a few notes. He had interviewed both parties about the car accident. It seemed that one car had careered from one side of the road to the other and had luckily hit another car sideways on. No one was seriously injured. One driver had jarred his neck and was wearing a surgical collar, the other had fractured his elbow.

The car that had lost control had recently been purchased from Whytfield Motors, and the driver was in his mid-forties. He maintained that he hadn't been speeding and that the steering had failed as he rounded a bend in the road. Police experts had examined the car and noticed the omission of the chassis number. It was assumed that the car was older than the registration document listed. Wilkins recounted his findings to Stagg.

"So, he sells these cars at a bargain price, claiming they're younger than they actually are?"

"Yes, sir. He must get older cars from somewhere and swap the number plates over."

"Yes, clever. I've heard of them doing this up in Liverpool."

"Yes. You wouldn't think they'd do this sort of thing round here, though, would you?"

"I keep telling you, Wilkins, crime is everywhere. Where there are people, there's crime."

"Well, thank goodness there are more good people than bad, sir." Wilkins smiled.

"Indeed." Stagg couldn't help but smile himself. "We'd better pay Whytfield Motors and Mr Jack Evans another visit, I think."

Stagg and Wilkins discovered that Barry had left the garage and got a job at Wenbury and that Jan Brooks had also left.

"To be honest, it wasn't long after you came here," said Jack Evans.

"I see," said Stagg. "Could I have another word with your other mechanic, please?"

"Tony? Yes of course. I'll just shout him for you now."

The mechanic came into the showroom wiping his hands on a greasy rag.

"Now, I want to know whether you knew anything about these cars that Barry was doing up and registering to this garage," Stagg said sternly.

"You what? To here? No, they wouldn't do that. You wouldn't do that, would you, Tony?" Jack Evans shouted.

"No, I haven't. I don't know anything about it."

"You're sure? Only someone's been injured," Stagg persisted.

"Injured? No, it's nothing to do with me. I told Barry. He was doing up a few cars in his own time. You knew, Mr Evans, 'cos you said it was okay for him to use the garage."

"Yes, it was only supposed to be for small jobs. I didn't say register them to this garage, did I? Bloody cheek, that is!" He glared at the mechanic.

"I tell you, Mr Evans, I didn't know anything about that. He did the cars up, and, well, I'm not sure if it was Jan who registered them. He seemed to like talking to her a lot, in his breaks and that. All I do is come to work and go home. Only he was a bit greedy, I think, was Barry. That's all I know."

"I see, all right. Thank you," Stagg said to the mechanic.

"Well, it just goes to show you. You can't trust anyone, can you? My wife's right. Maybe I will sell up and retire to Spain." Jack Evans exclaimed.

"Thank you for your help, Mr Evans. Can you tell me Barry's address, please?" Wilkins asked. Jack Evans handed him a slip of paper with the details noted down.

"There! And I hope he gets what's coming to him. He won't be coming back here, that's for sure," he said with disgust.

CHAPTER 23

The next day, Stagg decided to send Wilkins to interview Barry about the cars. He wanted to check a few details in his office. Later, he decided to drive over to Monkton. He could pick up some more daffodil bulbs from the garden nursery there for Pamela.

On his way back to the station, he saw an Austin A40 car and remembered the caretaker he'd visited a while back. Stagg went to the village shop again for a newspaper, and the shop assistant recognised him at once.

"Ah, here again? Fry's chocolate, wasn't it?"

Stagg chuckled. "You have a good memory."

"Yes, I have. Now, wasn't it Harold Jones you were looking for?"

"Right again," said Stagg, getting some change out of his pocket.

"He's a nice chap, isn't he?"

"Yes, he is."

Stagg only had half a crown. The woman took the coin and opened the till.

"Sad about his daughter, though. Not that I'm a tittle-tattler, of course."

"Jennifer?" Stagg remembered.

"Yes. Just moved from here one day and didn't come back. I believe she phoned Harold to say she had a new life now, and he didn't feature in it. You know how these youngsters can be." She handed Stagg his change.

"She went off on her own?"

"Well," the woman leaned forward onto the counter, "she said she was on her own, but I reckon it was that boyfriend of hers. He used to come in here as cool as you like. Opening all the magazines and papers and leaving them all untidy. I told him, *"other people have to read them, you know,"* and he just laughed. He was horrible. Yellow teeth he had. I can't bear dirty teeth!"

"I see, and just refresh my memory, when was this?"

"Well, it must be two, no, three years ago, 'cos our Valerie had just been confirmed. Gosh, the time goes quickly, doesn't it?"

"Yes, it does. Thank you for the paper and the information."

"That's all right. You're very welcome. Please do call again," she called out as he left the shop.

Stagg got back in his car and glanced at the paper. Three years ago, the shopkeeper had said. He rubbed his chin, pondering a few moments before starting the car.

He pulled in front of the terraced house and glanced at the windows. They all had lace curtains, but Stagg could see that Mr Jones' were a bit dull, as if they hadn't been washed for some time. He checked his watch, and it was one o'clock, the same time that he'd called previously.

Stagg knocked on the door quietly, and Harold Jones opened it, holding a tea towel as before. Stagg assumed caretakers must like holding cloths.

"Oh, hello again. Everything all right?" Harold asked.

"Hello. Yes. I'd just like a word, Mr Jones, if that's all right."

"Well, no, actually, it isn't. I told you, I don't know anything. Now, if you don't mind." He tried to close the door, but Stagg put his hand against it.

"Can I just check on the cyanide you still have, Mr Jones?"

"Oh, all right, if you must. Don't worry; it's still in the shed." He trailed back through the house to the back door and unlocked the shed. "See, here. It's in this old tin. There!" He held an old Brasso tin up before Stagg.

"Yes, I see. Thank you, Mr Jones. That's all right. I've seen enough, thank you." Stagg watched as the caretaker carefully stored the tin on the top shelf of his shed. The package was unopened. "So, you haven't used any of it yet, Mr Jones?"

"No, not yet. To be honest, I don't like using it. There was only a small nest, so I smashed it up with a broom handle."

"I see. Thank you, Mr Jones."

Stagg drove back to the station, his mind in a whir. He knew he should have asked Harold for a full statement. It was only his record of events, after all. He could have had two packets of cyanide. But the poor man had been put through enough, surely?

To do nothing went against everything that Stagg had been trained for as a police officer.

Stagg thought of Pamela Hudson, his dear Pamela, and what the Brooks brothers had put her through. At the same time, Stagg believed in justice, and he still hadn't established who had killed Charley Brooks.

Back at the station, he contacted the Education Department to check how many packets of cyanide had been issued to Harold Jones and was relieved when they confirmed that it was just one. He wrote up his report quickly and slammed his desk drawer shut. He'd put it on file tomorrow. He got up, put on his coat, and left the station. He wanted to visit Nora Davies.

***

Nora had been allowed to come home from hospital, but her parents had had strict instructions for Nora to do exercises. These would improve her muscles and tendons and would prevent her from walking with a limp. Stagg had kept in regular touch with her parents and knew they would take the hospital instructions very seriously. He decided to call in at the local sweet shop and pick up a Christmas treat for Nora.

Stagg knocked gently on the door of the little cottage and waited. He felt a bit self-conscious, holding a large box of chocolates, and was glad when Mrs Davies opened the door.

"Oh, hello! Come in. Lovely to see you, sir." She stepped back to allow Stagg into the house.

"I just thought I'd pop and see how Nora's getting on. I've brought her an early Christmas treat. I hope that's all right?"

Mrs Davies looked at the large box of chocolates and smiled. "Gosh, Nora will be so pleased. It's such a big box of chocolates!"

Nora was propped up against two pillows in an armchair, and her sister Josie sat near her. They had been drawing some pictures, but when Stagg entered, Josie hastily pulled them off the bed.

Mrs Davies said, "Come on now, tidy those away. Mr Stagg has come to see you, Nora."

Stagg perched on the arm of a chair. "These are for you, Nora, for being such a brave girl." Nora smiled at the picture of a rose bouquet on the box adorned with a large pink ribbon.

"They're all for me?" she whispered.

"Yes, all for you, unless you know someone you'd like to share them with, of course."

Stagg moved away from her, and Josie stepped forward. He watched Nora pull at the ribbon and open the box. She picked out a chocolate and quickly popped it into her mouth. Then she took another one and ate that.

Her sister watched her but said nothing until Nora said, "Do you want one? They're very nice." She took another one and munched away. She was clearly enjoying herself.

Her sister said, "Yes, please. Which ones are the orange ones? I like orange chocolates."

Stagg and Mrs Davies left the girls studying the chocolates' descriptions.

"Thank you so much, Mr Stagg. You're very kind for remembering Nora."

"And how is she getting on with her exercises?"

"Well, she doesn't like picking up marbles with her toes very much, but the doctors say it stretches the tendons, so she has to do it. She's walking now. She has to take her time, but she's getting better each day."

"Good. I'm glad she's coming on." Stagg smiled.

"Yes. Thank you. I'd better go back in, or they'll make themselves sick. Thanks again."

Stagg got back in his car and saw Nora in the window, waving and smiling. He waved back and then drove back to the station. He saw little point in telling the Davies that it was more than likely that their daughter had been hit by the Brooks brothers. They had probably used the lane as a shortcut on their way back from committing the robbery at the Baines factory.

The next morning, Burns appeared at Stagg's doorway.

"What's this I hear about you harassing Mr Baines, Stagg?"

"Sir? I simply asked him a couple of questions, hardly harassment."

"Be careful, Stagg, that's all. I don't like my friends complaining to me about my officers." He wandered down the corridor, shaking his head. Stagg said nothing. His phone rang, and it was the chief.

"Stagg? Just thought I'd let you know that Wilkins has been given a special award for rescuing Hudson. It'll be presented at the Christmas Ball."

"I see. Good. I must congratulate him."

"Yes. He did very well, indeed. Oh, and Stagg?"

"Yes, sir?"

"You've been nominated too. Maybe bring Hudson with you. That's all for now."

Stagg replaced the receiver and smiled. He knew Wilkins would be impressed. Stagg wondered if Pamela would like to go to the Christmas Ball and realised he sounded like the prince or someone from a Cinderella pantomime. He had never been to the annual event, as he preferred to keep a low profile and out of the chief's way. Still, it'd be a night out, he mused. Perhaps he'd ask Pamela later.

Stagg had enjoyed seeing Hudson every night since her rescue, and they had just chatted over a cup of tea. Her mother had left them to it in the front room, busying herself in the kitchen. Stagg had been surprised at how easy Pamela Hudson was to talk to. She seemed to be getting on all right, but he knew it would take time for her to get over her ordeal. Whenever he saw her, he felt like wrapping his arms around her. He hoped that she would be able to forget it, but he knew this was unlikely.

CHAPTER 24

At Pamela's that night, after two cups of tea, Pamela decided to show Stagg where she'd been planting up daffodil bulbs ready for the spring. It was a dry evening, and she showed him how she'd bedded in the bulbs and planted a few primroses on the top.

"I've been keeping myself busy. It's a bit late to plant them, but they'll look lovely when they all come out. Thanks for bringing me some more." She beamed up at him.

"That's okay. Yes. They certainly will look nice."

Stagg thought how lovely she looked, her cheeks pink from the fresh air. It was nice to see her smile, as she hadn't smiled too much since her return home. Her long, dark hair waved down her back as she strolled beside him. She seemed relaxed. There was so much Stagg wanted to say to her, but he didn't want to rush things, not with Hudson.

Yet when he thought of what could have happened in that old station, his blood ran cold. He was sure she hadn't told him everything yet. She had said that the drug tests had revealed she had been given a strong sort of narcotic. The coroner had said it was a good job that she was carrying a bit of weight, or it could have had a worse effect. Stagg thought her weight was just as it should be.

They reached the potting shed, and Hudson wanted to show him some pansies she'd bought. She stepped inside to get them, but as Stagg stepped in, he caught his head. "Blast it!"

"Oh, are you all right?" Hudson swirled around and almost bumped into him in the small space. She moved his hand where he was holding his head. "Let's have a look. Well, the skin's not broken."

She was very close to his face. He looked down at her through his dark eyelashes and slowly lifted his hand to her cheek. She lifted her face to his, trying to see into his eyes but couldn't. She felt his lips brush hers, gently at first, then his arms tightened around her. She pulled away from him a little, surprised, and his arms dropped to his side.

"Sorry, I shouldn't have done that." He blushed. Hudson moved a little towards him.

"Why shouldn't you? I have wanted you to kiss me for a long time."

Stagg pulled her to him and kissed her deeply. She placed her head on his shoulder and he stroked her hair. He wanted her to stay with him forever, where she was safe.

The following day, he popped into the florist shop to buy her some flowers as a surprise. He'd decided to ask her to accompany him to the Christmas Ball. When he drove into Hudson's street, he was dismayed to find Burns' car parked outside her house. His heart crashed about in his chest, and fury bubbled up.

Hudson was just out of sight, in the doorway, and she was talking to Burns. He was giving her some flowers and seemed to be chatting to her in a friendly fashion from the way he was smiling. Stagg quietly reversed his car out of sight and parked further down the road. Burns continued chatting, so Stagg turned his car around and went home.

Stagg went into his garden and tore into some weeding for a bit. He didn't even change his clothes, and when he went into his shed and flung the garden fork down with a clatter, some seed trays fell off the shelves. Stagg sighed, slammed the door, and went inside his house.

He didn't visit Hudson for a few days and kept himself busy at work, staying in the station until after six. He missed Hudson a lot, and the thought of her brought bittersweet emotions. Burns hadn't helped the situation by telling him what a great girl Hudson was, as if Stagg didn't know that!

A few evenings later, Wilkins tapped on his door.

"Is everything all right, sir?"

"Yes, Wilkins. Why wouldn't it be?" Stagg didn't look up.

"Well, it's just that you seem to be working till late a lot recently. Is there anything I can do to help?"

"No, nothing, Wilkins. Thank you."

"I see." Wilkins coughed, and Stagg looked up.

"Is there something else, Wilkins?"

"Well, no, not really. I was just wondering how Hudson was getting on, sir."

"I'm sure she's getting on well, Wilkins."

"I was wondering whether I could go to see her, sir. Diane…sorry, WPC Jones said she hadn't looked very well yesterday when she'd visited."

"She's ill? Why didn't you tell me before, Wilkins?" Stagg stood up, and for a moment, Wilkins thought the inspector was going to hit him.

"She just said she looked under the weather, sir. I think I'll go to see her tonight. Shall we go together?" Wilkins eyed his boss thoughtfully.

"Yes, we will, Wilkins. In fact, it's six-fifteen, so we'll go now."

When Wilkins quietly knocked on Hudson's door, he heard someone running down the hall, and Hudson flung open the door.

"Oh, Wilkins. It's you." Wilkins saw the light of hope die in her eyes but smiled at her warmly.

"I thought I'd pop in to see my favourite WPC. How are you, Hudson?" Hudson stepped aside to let Wilkins in, holding onto the door.

"I'm well, thank you. Come in," she said politely. She tried to close the door, but something was stopping it. "Strange. What's stopping this door? Oh!"

"Any room for another visitor?" Stagg asked quietly.

"Adam Stagg! I thought you'd forgotten me!" Hudson flung her arms around him, hoping for a kiss, but she was greeted with a polite smile. "Whatever's the matter?" she said brightly.

"Nothing, Hudson. I'm pleased to see you're looking better."

"Oh! Yes, thank you. Well, come in. I'll make some tea." She showed the two men into the lounge, and they sat down.

"She looks well, doesn't she, sir?" Wilkins ventured. He noticed that Stagg was nervously gripping each of his fingers in turn.

"Yes, she does."

Hudson entered with a tray holding three mugs of tea, sugar, and some ginger biscuits.

"Here we are. Please, help yourself."

Wilkins took his mug and took a drink. "I'm glad to see you're better, Hudson. We were a bit worried about you, weren't we, sir?"

Hudson looked at Stagg, but he kept his gaze downwards. "Yes, we thought we'd better check up on you. Wilkins said he was going to visit you tonight, so I thought I'd accompany him. I hope you don't mind.'"

"No, of course not." Hudson looked into her mug.

Wilkins suddenly stood up. "Gosh! I've just remembered, I was supposed to be taking my mother to her bridge club. Sorry, but I must dash. Sorry, sir, see you tomorrow." He darted out before they had a chance to say goodbye.

"Maybe I should be going myself. Thank you for the tea."

"Oh! Must you? I haven't seen you for ages." Hudson smiled. "Thank you for coming." Hudson sat back down. "Is it busy at the station, Adam?"

"You know how it is, usual stuff.'"

"Yes. And how is the wonderful Inspector Burns?" Hudson rolled her eyes and chuckled, but her smile vanished when she saw Stagg's face. "What's the matter? I was joking. What is it, Adam?"

"What was he doing here?" Stagg growled.

"Who?"

"Burns! I saw him laughing and joking with you last week!"

"Oh! He asked me whether I remembered anything about my ordeal with Charley Brooks, and then he asked me to go to the Christmas Ball with him. Cheeky blighter! I told him I expected his wife would like to go with him, not me. I don't think he was very impressed. Big-headed so-and-so!" She chuckled at first, but then she stopped. "You surely didn't think I was interested in him, did you? Because I'm most certainly not. You do know that, don't you, Adam?" She gently put her hand in his. Stagg pulled her to him and kissed her deeply. "What was that for?" she eventually asked.

"For being so wonderful, Hudson. Will you come with me to the Christmas Ball, my lady?" asked Stagg.

"Yes, kind sir. Indeed, I will." Hudson laughed, and they had a very enjoyable evening together.

Pamela Hudson was thrilled at the thought of going to the Christmas Ball with Stagg. She was feeling a lot better now, and her bruises were fading. The minor burns she'd received were almost healed, but sometimes she'd still experience a feeling of being watched, and it made her shiver. She'd had no further nightmares about monkeys and tried to block them out of her mind. Some nights though, she'd wake up in a cold sweat, and all she could see were the iron window bars of the old station. She hoped these would pass, as she wanted to get back to work. She was grateful for her mother's attention and care, but she wanted to be out and about, whereas her mother expected her to sit under a blanket on the sofa all day, drinking cups of tea.

The Christmas Ball! She wondered whether she should wear a mini dress or a long one. How should she wear her hair? Up or down? She'd ask Diane, WPC Jones, who always attended this event. She'd know, for sure. Hudson hadn't been to a police party as she had never been asked by any male officers, and she hadn't wanted to be a wallflower. No, this time was going to be special, she could tell. She felt a surge inside when she thought of Stagg and smiled. It was going to be a lovely Christmas.

CONCLUSION

The following day, Stagg was in a very good mood. He even smiled at one of the WPCs in the corridor.

Burns appeared at his doorway.

"Going to the Christmas Ball, are you? What's happened to you, Stagg? I must have missed something in that brunette you rescued. I'll have to have a dance with her myself if she performs miracles!"

Stagg crumpled up a piece of paper he held under his desk and wished it was Burns' neck.

"No, Hudson is going to be my partner for the whole of the evening."

"I hope she knows what she's letting herself in for, poor girl! What do you think, Wilkins?"

Wilkins, who had also appeared, said, "I'm sure Inspector Stagg will look after WPC Hudson, sir."

"Huh! And what would you know? Uncle's pet!" Burns snapped and sauntered down the corridor.

Wilkins sat down. "I know I shouldn't comment, sir, but I'm not keen on the assistant chief. He's not a good policeman, if you ask me."

"You're right, Wilkins." Wilkins' eyebrows shot up, and Stagg continued, smiling. "You shouldn't comment."

Stagg's phone rang.

"Stagg here...Yes, that's correct…Yes, Charles Brooks…When was that? Three years ago? I see, sir…Yes. Several cases involving those people I discussed with you the other day…I see…Yes, sir. I'll let the chief know immediately, sir, so he may phone you just to confirm…Yes, and thank you again, sir…Goodbye." Stagg leant forward and clasped his hands together.

Wilkins asked, "Everything all right, sir?"

"Splendid, Wilkins. Just splendid! Can you go over to see whether Jan Brooks will come into the station? We need to get a statement from her about those cars. I'll let you complete that report to close the case off, Wilkins."

"Yes, sir. Thank you."

***

The next few days were very busy for Wilkins and Stagg. Wilkins managed to get a statement from Jan Brooks and Barry, the mechanic, who first both blamed each other and then Charley Brooks. Wilkins recorded both statements and produced a very conclusive report.

It showed that they were all complicit in the illegal car dealings, and much to the relief of Jack Evans, it also stated he had no knowledge of this illegal operation which was going on right under his nose.

Once he'd handed the report to Stagg, Wilkins asked, "Sir, is it all right if I pop out for an hour?""

"Wilkins, we're very busy, as you know, and you want to pop out? Why, man?"

Wilkins blushed. "Well, the thing is, WPC Jones has had kittens. That is to say, her cat has, and I was wondering...."

"Yes, Wilkins? Can't you sort this after work?" Stagg snapped.

"Well, yes, sir, I could. I was going to take one for Mrs Morris to replace Kip, sir."

Stagg looked up from his paperwork and surprised Wilkins with a smile.

"Good idea, Wilkins! What colour is it?"

"It's a marmalade cat, just like old Kip, only smaller, of course. A right ball of fluff too!"

"Okay, but don't be too long, will you, or you'll miss all the fun."

"Sir?"

"I'll explain later. Off with you, now."

***

Mrs Morris was delighted with her kitten.

"Oh, he's lovely, John! I must admit, I've been missing old Kip. Now, what are we going to call you, my boy?" They both laughed as the kitten attacked an old ball of wool, rolling over and over. "I think I'll call him Ginger. Yes. He's Ginger. Thank you, John. Do you want a piece of apple pie? It's fresh today?"

"No, thank you, Mrs Morris. I have to get back to the station. I'm sorry."

"I'll pop a couple of pieces in a bag for you and the nice inspector for later. Busy today, is he?"

"Yes, he is. That would be lovely, thank you, Mrs Morris."

Wilkins waved goodbye and carefully laid the food on his front seat. He drove quickly back to the station and hoped he hadn't missed anything important. He knew Stagg had been very busy with paperwork and phone calls this week. He hoped he was pleased with the reports he'd given him this morning.

There was a buzz of excitement when Wilkins got back at the station. It seemed that, at Stagg's instigation, Birmingham Central police station had conducted their own investigation on two officers who had worked for Burns. They had admitted to taking bribes from criminals and drug-related offences involving Burns and Charley Brooks. Burns had been arrested.

Wilkins was later informed that the chief himself had taken a phone call about Burns from Mr Baines, the factory owner, and it had been quite illuminating.

Baines had employed Charley Brooks as a cheap courier of wares to Birmingham. That part of the scheme was all above board. What Baines hadn't known was that his wares were concealing drugs and were being transported in and out of the city. When Charley Brooks had boasted about being a business acquaintance of the assistant chief inspector, Mr Baines was surprised. He'd told the chief that Charley Brooks had become more demanding.

"I told him I didn't want him to do any more jobs for me, and then I was robbed. I'm ruined! Ruined!"

It was certainly a shock for the chief, too. Nevertheless, he obtained an emergency warrant for a police swoop on Burns' house while Burns was at the station. This had revealed the missing packet of cyanide from the Baines factory, which had been carefully hidden in his garage. There were also several tiny packages of heroin and cocaine.

A hand-writing expert had confirmed that the letter Charley Brooks had received had been written by Burns, even though he'd tried to disguise it. The police had discovered a donkey jacket and a dark, woolly hat, which could have been used in Wilkins' assault.

Assistant Chief Inspector Burns had been arrested at the station, much to everyone's surprise. It seemed that all the cases he'd 'cracked' in Birmingham had been set up. Burns had even been involved in some drug dealing himself, and a certain Charley Brooks had been supplying and collecting.

Burns was questioned by Stagg and the chief inspector, who'd asked whether he had been blackmailed by Charley Brooks.

"No comment."

The chief leaned forward. "You're not doing yourself any favours, Andrew. Now come on, tell us the connection between you and Brooks."

"No comment."

The chief banged his fist on the table. "We have indisputable evidence, Burns!"

"Indisputable evidence? What's that, for God's sake? Has that WPC been talking? Unreliable, she is! And I bet you planted the so-called evidence, didn't you, Stagg?" He pointed at Stagg and gave him a cold stare.

"No, I did not! And why would WPC Hudson know anything about you? Not unless you had links with Charley Brooks, after all. But I have other evidence, Mr Burns, which shows that you were involved in distributing and supplying drugs."

"I'll believe that when I see it! You surely can't believe these allegations that Stagg is making towards me, can you, Chief? I'm the best officer you've ever had. You told me so yourself!"

The chief ignored this remark and leant forward. "Were you being blackmailed by Charley Brooks?"

"And why would I be blackmailed by someone like him? He was just small fry! You really have no idea, have you?" Burns took out a cigarette and lit it. After a long drag of smoke, he sighed. "Ok. I'll do a deal with you. I have a lot of contacts that could be very useful to you." He drew on his cigarette again as if it was going to be his last one.

The chief said, "Look, Burns, I don't know whether you think you're above the law because you're not! You'd better come clean about it all. If you make a statement today listing all these contacts, maybe the judge will be lenient, but he may not. And murder is a serious charge, as you know!"

"But I solved all those cases in Birmingham. It was me! The other officers there are lying because they're just jealous of me!" Burns snorted.

He turned angrily to Stagg. "And you! You're just as bad. Pathetic, I call it! You can't pin this on me. It's that caretaker who killed him, not me!"

"What caretaker, Burns?" asked the chief.

"The one that Stagg interviewed. It was his daughter who'd overdosed, remember? Revenge it was, and he had access to cyanide."

"And how do you know his daughter was linked to Charley Brooks? Because I didn't file that report," Stagg asked.

The chief's eyebrows raised a little, and Burns shouted, "Yes, you did! You always follow procedure, especially after you lost that book years ago."

"Oh, the book that Betty stole from the station, as instructed by Charley Brooks. Yes, she's also confirmed that you assisted in the Brooks robberies by alerting them to police car movements. I know all about your dealings, Burns, and so does the chief."

"You don't know anything. You're a waste of space like your father was. A drunken failure! I remember seeing him at the golf club, trying to escape his humdrum life, and how did he end up, Stagg? Dead!" Stagg sprang up from his chair, but the chief held him by his arm.

"Sit down, Stagg! Now, Burns, my advice to you is to come clean and tell us all about it. You're not doing yourself any favours, man."

"I'm not saying anything else until my solicitor is present." Burns leant back in his chair and finished his cigarette.

"Very well. This interview is over. Sergeant, if you please?" The policeman escorted his ex-boss to a police cell.

Whilst the chief inspector had initially been as shocked as everyone else over Burns' conduct, he was glad that all this mess was over before Christmas and, more importantly, the Christmas Ball.

***

Pamela had been chatting about the Christmas dress her mother was going to make her for a few weeks now, and while Stagg had seen the paper pattern they had bought from Woolworths, he wasn't allowed to see the finished article until the night of the dance.

Pamela tried on the dress, and of course, it fitted perfectly. Her Mum had done a splendid job. They'd chosen a bottle-green velvet which complimented her dark hair perfectly. It was a simple cut, fitted, with a scooped neck and long sleeves. Pamela borrowed her mum's golden sandals and clutch bag. She looked in the wardrobe mirror and had to admit that she looked very smart indeed.

Her dark hair had been pinned up, and she had curled the tendrils at the side of her face. She sprayed a little of her California Poppy perfume that her mum had bought her the previous Christmas. There! She glanced at her watch, and it was seven-fifteen. Adam would be arriving soon, so she went downstairs.

The doorbell rang just as she came down, and Mrs Hudson opened the door. Stagg stepped in, and Pamela caught her breath when she saw him. His hair was combed back and was thick and smooth. He wore a tuxedo, as the dress code was black tie. He greeted Mrs Hudson and stopped in his tracks when he saw her daughter on the stairs. Their eyes met, and he extended his hand.

"My lady?" And they both laughed.

Wilkins was already at the local hotel where the police ball was held. He spotted Stagg and Hudson as soon as they arrived and watched many fellow officers give them admiring glances. He was going to get up and greet them, but his mother told him to sit back down as they were sitting at the chief's table. So, Wilkins waved at Hudson, who waved back, and Stagg, following her gaze, nodded to him. The music started, and the evening began.

After about an hour, when the dancing was in full swing, Wilkins appeared at Stagg's table.

"Hello. Would you like a drink?" Wilkins asked somewhat merrily.

"No thanks, we've just got one," Hudson said. Wilkins noticed she and Stagg were holding hands on the table.

"The food's supposed to be nice here, isn't it?" said Wilkins.

Stagg said, "I don't know, I haven't been here before."

"Oh! No, nor me. Well, I expect it's better than the police canteen, anyway. Would you like to dance?"

Hudson smiled. “No, thank you. We’ve just had a dance, haven’t we? And I think all my dances are booked for tonight.” She leaned a little against Stagg and squeezed his hand.

Wilkins was going to say how lucky Stagg was when the music suddenly stopped, and it was announced that *“Dinner was served!”*

The evening was a long one, but for Hudson, it was a lovely one. She had felt so proud to accompany Adam Stagg, especially when he’d accepted his award. She’d clapped so hard her hands ached and laughed when Wilkins had gone up onto the stage the wrong way to get his award. Good old Wilkins!

When they arrived at her house, she asked Stagg in for a nightcap. After several kisses, they sipped their brandies quietly. It had been a long day.

Hudson said, “What a nice night we’ve had. I really enjoyed it. Thank you for asking me, Adam.”

“No problem. It was my pleasure.” Stagg took another sip of his brandy. “The thing is, Pamela….”

Pamela Hudson put her finger on his lips. “No, don’t say it. I don’t want to spoil the evening.”

“You don’t know what I was going to say!” Stagg sat forward in his chair.

“Yes, I do. You were going to say something like you want us to be just friends. I know.” She reached forward for a drink, and Stagg took her glass from her hand and put it on the table. “I’m right, aren’t I? I knew it. And it’s been such a lovely night.” Hudson insisted.

Stagg sighed, then gripped both of her hands. "No, you're not always right, you know, Pamela Hudson. I'm disappointed." He looked deep into her dark eyes.

"Disappointed?" she whispered.

"Yes. You're wrong. I don't want us to be just friends. I love you. Will you marry me?"

"Yes, Adam," Pamela gasped. "Yes, please."

The following summer, Wilkins was the best man at Stagg's wedding. They walked up the stone path to Whytfield church, and as Wilkins nervously talked about his best man's speech, Stagg noticed someone putting flowers on one of the graves in the churchyard. It was Harold Jones.

Later, when Pamela Hudson arrived, her bouquet consisted of pink roses from Stagg's garden, and he had to admit that, for once, they were every bit as beautiful as his grandads had been.

ACKNOWLEDGEMENTS

Firstly, I would like to thank my husband for reminding me to eat and for listening to my relentless conversations about Stagg and Hudson. His patience and encouragement have been wonderful throughout the process.

I'd also like to thank my family and friends for their support, particularly Dr Kathy Hopewell, who helped me so much in my initial writing journey with Inspector Stagg. I'm also grateful to Fiona Knowles-Holland and Peter Jones, who have reviewed this book.

Thanks to Michelle Catanach for her brilliant design of the book cover, and last but not least, thanks to Estelle Maher and all the team at TAUK Publishing. You have helped me make this publication possible.

My sincerest thanks to all.

ABOUT THE AUTHOR

SW Fellows enjoys writing about romance, comedy, murder and mystery, which can be a tricky combination!

She was born and bred in North Wales and still enjoys its wonderful culture, weather, and stunning landscapes. Her interests have always been torn between art and writing, and she enjoys sketching and composing some very questionable watercolours.

In university, she researched Agatha Christie, Dorothy L Sayers, and Margery Allingham. It was hard work, but how could she not enjoy all this cosy crime? The name 'Whitfield' cropped up in family genealogy, and SW Fellows decided to adapt this name into the fictional Shropshire town of Whytfield, where she reveals that everyone has their own tale to tell. SW Fellows has now retired from 'proper' work. She is, however, really keen to start her next Whytfield chapter….

CONNECT WITH SW FELLOWS:

Website: swfellows.co.uk
Facebook: SW Fellows author
Twitter: @SWFellowsAuthor

BOOKS BY THE AUTHOR (SO FAR):

The Whytfield Inheritance
The Whytfield Investigation

Printed in Great Britain
by Amazon

22486464R00137